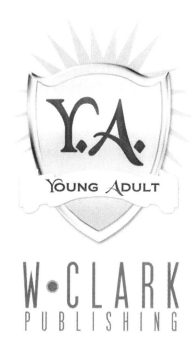

PLAYER HATER

A YOUNG ADULT NOVEL BY

CHARMAINE WHITE

D1113865

This is a work of fiction. Names, characters, places, and incidents either are the product of the author's imagination or are used fictitiously, and any resemblance to actual persons, living or dead, business establishments, events, or locales is entirely coincidental.

Wahida Clark Presents Young Adult
60 Evergreen Place
Suite 904
East Orange, New Jersey 07018
973-678-9982
www.wclarkpublishing.com
www.wcpyoungadult.com

Player Hater
ISBN 13-digit 978-1-936649-34-1
ISBN 10-digit 1936649349
Library of Congress Catalog Number 2012913337
  1. Young Adult, Contemporary, Urban Fiction, African
     American, – Fiction

Cover design by Nuance Art nuanceart@gmail.com
Interior book design by Nuance Art nuanceart@gmail.com

Printed in United States
Green & Company Printing and Publishing, LLC
www.greenandcompany.biz

WAHIDA CLARK PRESENTS

Y.A.
YOUNG ADULT

W·CLARK
PUBLISHING

PLAYER
HATER

A YOUNG ADULT NOVEL BY
CHARMAINE WHITE

DEDICATION

For all the Torean's in the world; without you guys, my life would be very lackluster.

ACKNOWLEDGEMENTS

First and foremost, I would like to thank God for blessing me with this opportunity. Next, I would like to thank Wahida Clark for working closely with me throughout this process as well. I would like to acknowledge my parents Aston and Kishah Walters, and Michael and Toya White.

Every single one of you has been constructive in my life, and without you all, I would not be where I am today. There are lots of people who have come into my life, provoking me to take bits and pieces of their traits to create my characters. For all of you, thank you for inspiring me. And thank you for all of the other inspirations to come.

ALLEN RIVERA
Thursday, 10:20am ~ SPANISH II

Allen sat in his cold, metal chair, banging his pencils against his desk to the fast beat of Drake's latest song. The only thoughts in his mind were about the empty seat in front of him and getting out of class as soon as possible so that he could get to lunch because he was starving. Already speaking fluent Spanish, Allen personally found Spanish II a waste of his time, but needing two credits to graduate, the stupid high school had him stuck there until the end of the semester.

"Yo', Allen!" a tall boy said as he made his way into the Spanish II classroom.

"What's good?" Allen replied, taking his eyes off his pencils to look at the boy.

"I caught your roast last night on YouTube. That stuff about Ciara not knowing how to sing was hilarious!"

The group of kids who were already in the room shouted their forms of agreement to Allen.

"Thanks man, you know I gotta speak the truth on these things bro."

"Fa sho', fa sho'," the tall boy replied, giving Allen dap before taking his seat.

Allen posted comedy roasts about celebrities every Wednesday night, and almost all the kids from Wilson watched them. Allen Rivera was the funny man, the class clown of Wilson High. He knew how to keep his fans laughing and gained their respect for doing it. Allen was straight up FUNNY, and that was what everyone loved about him.

Caught off guard, Allen jumped at the sudden blare of the tardy bell. While in his zone, thinking of something funny to say about the incident, Torean Hudson interrupted him.

"Aye Al, anyone sittin' in this seat?" Torean asked, pointing to the vacant chair on the right side of Allen.

Allen looked up at Torean, raised his eyebrows, and said, "Are you blind man? Do you not see my dude Tim sitting right next to me?"

"What the heck are you talkin' 'bout?"

Allen's brown eyes got big and he said, "Oh! My bad Torean, you probably can't see him 'cause the dude's so white that he's practically invisible. Here," Allen acted like he was kicking someone out of the chair and finished, "Alrightee then, the seat's empty now."

Torean laughed as he took his seat next to Allen, "Man, you are retarded!"

"What? Is it because I'm Mexican?" he pretended to be offended.

"Whatever man. But yo', I checked out your roast on Ciara last night. That video was hella funny. Especially the weave jokes!" Torean said, falling into a fit of laughter while remembering the show last night.

Allen gave Torean a play.

"You know I had to get her. That stuff is priceless. That chick be walkin' around with a new wig for every occasion."

The people who were close enough to hear him broke into laughter right when the teacher walked inside.

"Hey class, sorry I'm late. Well, I'm not really that sorry. Ha, ha!" Mr. Brunning, a short, pudgy, Asian man said, laughing at his own comment as he made his way into the Spanish II classroom five minutes past the tardy bell.

PLAYER 2 HATER

Torean rolled his eyes and mumbled to Allen, "Why does he think he can show his fat butt up to work any time he wants?"

"Yeah!" Allen shouted so that everyone in the room could hear, "Why come when students walk in tardy we go to detention, but when the teachers come through all extra late everybody's supposed to be cool with it?"

All the kids started laughing; trying to cover their laughter with their hands. Mr. Brunning hated it when Allen tried to get smart with him.

Blowing out some air in frustration, he rudely replied to Allen, clearly fed up with his attitude, "I figured no one in this class learns anything anyway, so I might as well take my time coming. It is not as if I am looking forward to seeing your faces on a daily basis. Ha, ha!" he bellowed while turning to the dry-erase board to write down the lesson for today.

Looking at Allen, Torean's face immediately turned slightly red as he started shaking with laughter. Just by looking at Allen, Torean knew what he was about to do next. Torean shook his head at Allen and quietly said, "Get 'em."

Allen pounded his fists on his desk and shouted, "Get yo big ha ha looking ass outta here."

"Get 'em!" this time Torean shouted, beginning to get excited.

Allen continues, "Get yo big Chinese ass tryna teach Spanish lookin' ass outta here!"

"GET 'EM!"

"Get yo big Mr. Miyagi lookin ass, yo big Chinese fried rice eatin' ass!"

Trying to ignore what Allen was saying, Mr. Brunning's face turned redder by the second by his frustrations. And to make matters worse, all the kids were laughing like crazy instead of coming to his rescue. Some of them were even crying from laughing so hard.

"Get yo bald headed ass outta here, lookin' like Mr. Clean!"

"Get 'em!"

"That's ENOUGH!" Mr. Brunning shouted, turning around to face Allen with spit flying out of his mouth with every word he spoke, "Get your hinnies up! You and Torean, get the heck out of my classroom!"

Torean and Allen slowly rose from their seats, "Okay, okay, Mr. China Man, no need to freak out," Allen said in a corny Chinese accent while raising his hands up in surrender.

As they left the classroom and headed toward the principal's office, they heard a ton of laughter down the hall and distinctly heard Mr. Brunning shout, "QUIET!"

When the two of them reached their destination, they sat on the small wooden bench, and waited.

"Now that was some funny stuff! You are hilarious!" Torean said to Allen while giving him a play.

Allen smiled, "That's me, the funny man."

"The ladies must love you."

Allen popped his collar like a big shot, saying, "Well you know. I do what I do."

Though Allen was funny, he couldn't solely depend on his jokes to get girls. Luckily for him, Allen's Latin ethnicity blessed him with a strong tan skin with not one blemish in sight. With the thickest, curliest hair, he was tall, lean, and had perfect white teeth, thanks to braces and Crest Whitening Strips. All of those attributes made Allen out to be a handsome guy.

As the two of them sat in front of the office waiting to be sentenced, a pretty, chocolate-skinned girl with the legs of a goddess walked past the two boys.

PLAYER ₄ HATER

"Dang!" they shouted out in unison while checking out the girl's butt.

Allen grabbed the girl by her wrist and pulled her back toward him, "Aye, can you let a brutha holla?"

The girl rolled her eyes at Allen and pulled her arm away, "Brutha? Boy please!" she stated as she walked away from the two of them.

"She wasn't that fine anyway," Allen mumbled while watching the girl walk away, feeling rejected.

Torean tapped Allen on the shoulder, "Let me show you how it's done."

"Hey lil' mama, can you come here for a second?" Torean shouted down the hallway to the sexy-legged girl.

The girl turned around, looked at Torean while pointing to herself, and mouthed, "Me?"

"Yeah you," Torean replied suavely.

Allen tissed in annoyance and mumbled to Torean, "Who else does she think you were talking to? Seriously."

The girl couldn't help but show all her teeth while she grinned from ear to ear on her way to the famous Torean Hudson. Once the girl came back over by the two guys, Allen watched the whole scene, trying to see what girls found so enticing about Torean. Allen couldn't deny the fact that this guy had swag. He had this creamy caramel complexion with piercing grey eyes. With his thin lips, low-cut wavy hair and fit frame, Torean, along with everyone else at Wilson High, knew he was one of the best-looking guys at the high school.

"Aye ma, I was just caught up in how fine you were and how sexy those legs looked while they were walking past me." Allen peeped Torean lightly run his finger down a short section of the girl's thigh.

She bit her lip, trying to settle her ecstatic smile, "Aww thanks."

"I was just wonderin' if I could get your number so that I can get to know you *and* those sexy legs. Maybe if I'm lucky, even what's between those legs, a little better," Torean finished while looking her up and down flirtatiously.

The girl, winked at Torean while she placed her number into his glossy cell phone.

"Thanks sexy," Torean said to the girl, while locking his phone and putting it back into his pocket.

"The ladies don't love a funny man. The ladies love *that*." Allen said after the girl was out of earshot from them.

Torean looked over at Allen and replied, "Well, I'm not the leader of the Clique Boys for nothin'."

Allen leaned his head against the wall of the office and dryly snorted at Torean's comment, "I guess you have a point there."

ALLEN RIVERA
Thursday, 6:38p.m. ~ HOME

It was six thirty-eight at night, and Allen sat at the small round table with his mom and dad, getting ready to chow down on dinner. Allen watched his mom place down his father's plate, and his stomach gave an excited grumble when he saw the delectable meal, he and his family were about to eat.

"Dang ma, you must be in a good mood today!" Allen said to his mother once his plate was placed in front of him. They were eating Picadillio, a traditional Mexican dish made of seasoned ground beef and peppers. Any other day Allen's mom would make pork chops or tacos, but for her to make such a time-consuming meal that looked as if it was made by his Abuela herself really took Allen off guard.

"Oh Allen, you act as if I never feed you guys," Rosalie responded to her son. She sat down at the table and placed her napkin on her lap, "Now I know I haven't made anything this special since your father got that new promotion at work, but you have to give me more credit than that."

Allen's mom was a soft looking woman with delicate features, resembling actress Thalia Ariadna. Rosalie had a thin frame, weighing 140 pounds and the same thick, curly hair as Allen, except it reached the middle of her back. Her tan skin had copper freckles, and a warm-hearted smile was usually settled on her face, but tonight her face was tight, showing a distinct sign of stress.

"Well Rosalie, this is a very great meal, and I cannot wait to start eating," Allen's dad said to his wife.

Allen's mother weakly smiled at her husband picked up her fork to eat, and right when she was about to put the food in her mouth, she dropped the fork, folded her arms, and looked up at Allen. His father moved around uncomfortably in his seat, sensing the storm that was quickly approaching.

"Allen Miguel José Martinez Rivera! What were you thinking? Getting sent to the office again?" Rosalie yelled across the table.

Oh, here we go again. Allen thought as he placed his fork down and looked up at his mom, waiting for her to finish shouting at him.

"Trece times! Tres veces esta semana Allen! Qué estás haciendo? Tratando de romper su propio record?"Allen's mom stood up and placed her hands on her hips. "Well are you going to speak? Or are you just gonna sit there looking stupid?"

"Ma, you don't understand! That Mr. Brunning treats all his students like crap, and I was just standing up for us. He deserved it!" Allen huffed. It wasn't fair that his mom was freaking out on him. It wasn't as if he vandalized Mr. Brunning's car; he only shouted out a few jokes. He couldn't help it if his way of defending himself was by making gags.

Allen's mom walked right up to where Allen sat and put her dainty finger in his face, "Do you think our family came to this country so that you can make jokes and get sent to the office every time I look around? No! Your father and I left Mexico twenty years ago so that we could make a better life for our children and ourselves. But it seems that the child I had did not truly appreciate all we did to get here!"

Allen looked over at his father, giving him a signal with his eyes to chime in at any moment to help him out.

"Rosalie, calm down," Allen's dad said to his wife, "Maybe the teacher really was being rude to the students and Allen was just defending himself," Allen's father motioned towards his plate, "Its dinner; let's just eat," Allen's dad always knew when to come to his rescue. Even though Allen's mother screamed, he was grateful that his father intervened before she issued his grounding sentence.

"Thank God." Allen said to himself after blowing out the air he was holding in his mouth the entire time his mom was shouting at him.

"Fine," Allen's mom said, once again taking her seat, "But I'm warning you Allen. You better be careful what you do from this day forward, or there won't be any more roasts on that YouTube, and I mean it."

"Sí mami," Allen responded, taking a huge forkful of Picadillio and stuffing it into his mouth. Allen heard that threat so many times that whenever his mother would threaten him with it, he would respond as if she was simply talking about the weather. They knew how much he loved making his comedy roasts; they would never take that away from him.

"So how are things going at work?" Allen's dad, who is an exact replica of Allen, except older, with graying hair and creased skin, asked.

Allen looked up at his father, "Everything's going great. We got a new shipment of iPhones and the manager said that the employees could get a 50% off discount, so I'm going to buy me one of 'em."

Loving electronics, Allen couldn't have asked for a better job than Radio Shack. The job was fun and he got the hottest gadgets before anyone else, and being in the North Side Mall, he was able to check out all the fine girls, which was a plus. The only downside to it was getting paid minimum wage.

"Well, that's good hijo. I was getting sick of you walking around with that Blackberry. Those things are so played out to me," Rosalie said, laughing while spooning some more food onto her plate.

Allen and his dad laughed, "Since when do you know so much about cell phones, Mom?"

"I know about *everything*," Rosalie spoke in an ominous tone.

His dad slowly nodded his head in agreement.

Allen rolled his eyes at his parents playfully. Even though he was always getting into trouble for being obnoxious at school, and his mom and dad took their role of good cop, bad cop much too seriously; Allen had to admit that he had some pretty great parents. They sacrificed a lot to come to America so that he could have the opportunity to live to his full potential, and Allen would always appreciate that. Along with comedy, family was his life. Without the two, Allen Rivera would not be anything near the person who he was today.

CHARMAINE WHITE

ALLEN RIVERA & TOREAN HUDSON
Friday, 2:15p.m.
SEVENTH HOUR /STUDENT ANNOUNCEMENTS

Torean and Allen stood in the video
production's classroom where they taped the morning
announcements for the next day. The two boys were looking
in the huge mirror on the back of the door, fixing the ties of
their suits. Everyone who was an anchor for the
announcements had to dress up for the class. Allen wore a
simple pair of grey dress pants with a white Oxford shirt,
cuffed at the sleeves, and a blue and grey striped tie. Torean
rocked a pair of blue jeans with a navy blue oxford shirt under
a white linen blazer. Both looked super good for the day's
announcements.

The two boys heard a soft tap on the door.

"Come in," Torean said, brushing his hair.

When the door opened, Allen's casual demeanor changed
as he started to get nervous.

"Hey guys, how much longer are you going to be, because
everyone's waiting on you," Carmen Sanchez, their co-anchor
said.

She looked over at Allen, who stared at himself in the
mirror awkwardly, and smiled, "Allen, you look fine. Can we
please just get started now? You guys know how much I hate
wearing these clothes," Carmen complained, yanking at her

silk shirt for emphasis. After giving the guys another quick grin, exposing her pearly whites, she exited the room.

Fixing his blazer, Torean said, "We *all* know how much she likes to get out of her clothes."

Allen playfully punched Torean in the arm, "Dude, do not even go there. Carmen's not like that at all."

"Oh, now you know how to speak? When Carmen was in here you couldn't speak two words, but now that she's gone, you wanna say something?"

Allen raised his eyebrows obliviously, "If I knew what you were talking about I would respond to what you just said; but I don't, so I'll just let that comment go." Allen went to open the door, but Torean held it shut.

"You know what I'm talkin' about Al. I notice everything that goes on around here, and I *definitely* know that you're feeling her."

Allen tissed, "I'm not feeling Carmen or whatever. She and I are just chill with each other. That's it."

Torean rolled his eyes, "Sure Al, say what you want."

Allen shook his head, turning down Torean's comment. Fixing his tie, Allen began to get annoyed at Torean all over again. First, he was acting like some all-seeing eye who knew that Allen was into Carmen, which was none of his business; and now Torean was breathing out these insanely loud, thick snores right in Allen's ear. Torean was seriously rubbing Allen the wrong way before he had to go out on set.

* * *

"Dang Torean, do you really need to breathe that hard?"

"What are you talking about?" Torean asked, his hand on the doorknob, preparing to leave the room.

"You're breathing like a fat—" Allen quickly moved Torean's hand from the doorknob, "Wait!" he whispered to

Torean. Allen put his ear to the door and heard the breathing again.

Guuuh guuuh ahhh guuuh

"Yo Torean, I think Lafonda is waiting outside this door," Allen said to his friend, panic in his voice.

Torean put his fist to his mouth to stop himself from laughing. Torean has heard stories about Lafonda Rice and her crush on Allen, but he didn't know that this girl was on stalker status.

Guuuh, guuuh, ahhh, guuuh

"Man, she's still out there!" Allen whispered. With his ear still pressed against the door, he heard the crinkling of plastic, "I think she's eating something."

Torean quickly put his ear to the door and listened.

"Mmmm, I love mey some Big Texus," Lafonda moaned on the other side of the door. Ten seconds after opening the pastry wrapper, Lafonda slid the empty package under the dressing room door.

Torean picked it up and began cracking up laughing. He tried handing it over to Allen, but once Allen saw the huge heart drawn in permanent marker on the Big Texas bag; he moved his body out of the way.

"Dude, that girl seriously gets on my nerves!" Allen whined.

"Well at least *someone* wants you," Torean joked.

Allen cut his eyes at Torean while he opened the door, "This stays between me and you."

The two of them left the dressing room and made their way into the media center. The room had a green screen and a long table with three chairs, one for Torean, Carmen, and Allen. A tripod with a camcorder stood a few feet in front of the table.

"Finally, you're here!" Kayla, a pretty girl, mixed with Native American and black with long, wavy, black hair and glasses, shouted when she saw the two boys arrive into the room. Kayla practically ran the student announcements. She hated it when her anchors showed up late because they wanted to stare at themselves all day long.

"Yes, yes, we're here Boss Lady," Allen joked, trying to forget about the creepy scene that just took place a few minutes ago, "Geeze Kayla, calm down; Harvard won't decline your acceptance if we don't film the announcements at exactly two-thirty."

Kayla laughed, "Shut up and let's just get this thing done."

Torean walked over to his seat at the long table, and his friend and fellow Clique Boy, Ricky Vega, who worked the cameras for the announcements, walked up to him. "What's good my man?" Ricky said to Torean.

Torean gave his boy a fist bump, "Nothin' much man. Just tryna get over this crazy hangover from last night's party."

"Oh yeah," Ricky said in agreement, "that party was crazy. The T.L.C.'s definitely know how to throw a bash!" Ricky reminisced on the blaring music, the countertops covered in hard liquor, and the coffee table littered in White Owl rappers. Parties around Wilson tended to get pretty wild, and this one was no different.

"Man, it was only the T.L.'s who threw the party, 'cause Carmen wasn't even there," Torean joked.

"What about me?" Carmen asked as she walked over to her seat next to Torean.

Ricky replied, "We were just talkin' about how your sexy butt wasn't at your girl's party last night."

Carmen rolled her eyes and put some lip gloss on her lips, "I had far better things to do on my Thursday night than to go to a party, even if it was my crew's, knowing that we had school the next day. Tiffany and Lauren were tripping, planning a party on a week night."

Torean bent his head into Carmen's face and said, "What better things did you have to do last night? Or should I say *who* did you have to do last night?"

Ricky and Torean laughed, and Carmen pushed Torean's head out of the way.

Allen walked up to the table right when he saw Torean in Carmen's face. He tried to let it go, but thoughts of the conversation the both of them had a few minutes back about his feelings for Carmen kept creeping on him.

"Hey Allen," Carmen smiled in his direction while he took a seat right next to her.

"Como está?" Allen said.

"Estoy muy bien," Carmen responded with another smile.

"Oh here we go again with the private Spanish conversations," Ricky said rolling his eyes sarcastically, "You guys do know that I'm Spanish too, right?"

"Whatever you whore," Carmen joked under her breath.

"If anyone's a whore here, it's you."

Allen tissed under his breath at Ricky; once again, there was a comment referring to Carmen as being a whore. The Clique Boys had nothing better to do than to throw dirt on someone's name. Allen believed that Carmen was not that type of girl at all. He just wished everyone else at Wilson would believe the same thing.

"Oh, here we go again Ricky! You're such a hater!" Carmen shouted, flipping her long hair in aggravation.

Kayla came up and broke up the heated discussion, "It's time to start the announcements guys."

"Fine by me," Torean replied, a hint of a smile on his face. He absolutely loved when people were arguing. It was as if he fed off the drama that Wilson High produced. Torean thought of himself as the all-seeing eye at Wilson, so he knew that Allen got bothered when Ricky called Carmen out, and he knew it was because Allen had a crush on her. All Torean had to do now was to make Allen admit it.

ALLEN RIVERA
Friday, 3:21p.m. ~ AFTERSCHOOL

"I am *too* happy the day is over," Allen said to his best friend Patrick as he leaned against the door of his four-year-old red Chevy pick-up truck.

"Isn't everybody?" Patrick replied, "I tell you bro, going to high school should be optional."

"For Sure!"

Allen gazed around the parking lot of the high school. Everyone stood around talking to their friends about whatever went down that day. Allen for one had a pretty sweet day. Mr. Brunning didn't show up to school, he didn't have any homework so he was able to go to sleep during his study hall class, and he could've sworn he saw Carmen checking him out while he was doing his segment of the announcements—not that he cared about what Carmen was looking at; he was not interested in her.

"They sure know how to get the boy's attention around here, don't they?" Patrick mumbled to Allen while his eyes were stuck on three of the most talked about girls in the boy's locker room at Wilson.

Allen couldn't help but stare.

The T.L.C.'s, which stood for the names of three sophomore girls by the names of Tiffany, Lauren, and Carmen, were most simply put, the sluts of Wilson High. They could easily put the Clique Boys to shame. They got triple the amount of admirers the Clique Boys did. They started so much more drama. And their impact had spread much further than the brick walls of Wilson High School, and had now engulfed the greater Madison area.

Tiffany Rodgers, the leader and H.B.I.C. of the group was every hood boy's fantasy. She had a cutthroat attitude, street smarts, and knew how to hold her own. With her smooth brown skin, micro braids, brown eyes, and big breast over a skinny frame, she knew how to work what she had, and was not ashamed of doing it. It was well known that just about any major, important person had given Tiffany Rodgers a test drive. From hood rich dope boys who loved to trick her off, to star high school, even college athletes; Tiffany had every guy eating out of the palm of her sassy hand.

Next, there was Lauren. Now, she was the tall glass of white milk of the group. Her creamy skin, blonde hair, blue eyes, skinny figure, and pouty lips gave her a very innocent look, but she was anything but innocent. The boys at Wilson went crazy for her. She had the whole "ditz" thing working for her and the guys at Wilson fell for it every single time.

And finally, there was Carmen. The sexy Latina. She was Puerto Rican with black glossy hair, big brown eyes, and was thick in all the right places. She was also a major flirt. Carmen knew how to get a guy to go all googley-eyed, and then hustle just about whatever she wanted from them. Unlike the rest of the girls, she didn't flaunt the fact that she was a freak behind closed doors; the title of her crew spoke for itself, and she didn't need to broadcast the fact that she could get every guy at school to be her bitch.

Although tried many times, the T.L.C.'s couldn't be touched by any wanna-be bad girl crew. They had their own style, and their sexiness spoke for itself. If there was a party going on, the T.L.C.'s were right in the middle of it. If a couple just broke up, Tiffany, Lauren, or Carmen had something to do with it. And if any one of the T.L.C.'s had a boyfriend, whoever that boy was had to have been the ish, the bomb, a ten, hell, a certified twenty. He had to be IT.

"Yo, Allen, you still here?" Patrick said to his friend, waving his hand in Allen's face to get his attention.

"Huh?" Allen replied, still checking out the girls, who were now making it into their separate cars.

Patrick huffed and shook his head, "Man, how many times am I going to have to tell you that Carmen is totally out of you league? I'm talking out of this galaxy."

"Yeah Pat and do you think she's in *your* league?" Allen replied sourly.

Patrick laughed while he ran has hand over his attractive face. Patrick had sexy tan skin and was muscular thanks to the varsity football team. He was tall, had short hair, and fierce, green eyes.

"Man dude, Carmen is not my type. I kinda like girls who haven't hooked up with half the guys on my team; let alone the entire school," Patrick said, leaning his back against the hood of Allen's truck. The parking lot was almost empty, except for the typical goodies who liked to stay after and study.

Allen rolled his eyes, "How many times am I going to have to tell people? I've known Carmen since elementary school, and we go to the same church; I don't think she's a whore like everybody says." Allen never experienced Carmen's bad side. Not being in the same circle that the T.L.Cs ran in, he didn't see her drinking, partying, and hooking up with multiple guys like Patrick did. All he's ever known was the sweet, funny girl who sat behind him every Sunday morning.

Patrick started to laugh, "Al! That girl's a slut. A ho. A skank. Straight up everything in the book. There's no way that girl can fool anybody. She opens her legs for any player who asks her to, and if you're too stupid to see that a girl like that wouldn't holler at you if you were the last comedian on Earth, well, I just feel sorry for you bro."

"What's that supposed to mean?" Allen said, offended, "The ladies love a comedian. You see how they always say, *'Oh Al, you're soooo funny! You are soooo adorable Allen!'* The ladies love me; they can't get enough of this guy."

"Yeah, Al, the ladies love you so much that you haven't had a girlfriend since 7th grade, and the only conversations you and Carmen have had since we started high school are when you two do the morning announcements, and those are scripted!"

Allen opened up his car door, preparing to leave. He was having enough of his boy dissing him for not being player enough to bag Carmen.

Patrick raised his eyebrows, "So you're about to leave?"

"What the heck does it look like I'm doing?"

"Oh, the funny man couldn't take a joke?" Patrick said, "Whatever man, I'll catch you tomorrow. Hopefully, by then you'll get that sick fantasy of you and Carmen actually hooking up out of your head."

Allen started the engine of his Chevy, "Peace."

Patrick walked away to his car, shaking his head and laughing.

Allen frowned at the back of his best friend's head. He hated how brutally honest Patrick could be at times. Every now and then, Allen wanted his friend to shut up, and today was most definitely one of those days. Talk of him and Carmen was all Allen heard today. He didn't know what bothered him more; the fact that he never admitted to liking Carmen, the fact that everyone just assumed that he was feeling her, or the fact that he knew that he didn't have any shot at getting Carmen Sanchez to be his girl even if he wanted to.

CHARMANE WHITE

As first hour started, the kids of Wilson High sat at their desk waiting for the familiar lyrics of the Black Eyed Peas' "Let's Get It Started" to blast from the television sets, for the student announcements.

"Wussup Wilson High, it's time for the morning announcements hosted by ya boy Torean."

"Me, Carmen."

"And don't forget about the Wilson High Spotlight with Allen Rivera."

The camera turned from Allen after he spoke and faced the two anchors, Carmen and Torean, for the news.

"The French Club is sponsoring a trip to Paris, France. Anyone who's interested may apply. The trip is estimated to cost one-thousand dollars, so if you're up for a good time, please contact Madame Fauve for more information." Torean announced.

"The Single's Dance is fast approaching, so everyone who's planning to go and get their party on needs to buy a ticket. Tickets will be sold during the break periods until the day before the dance. Hurry before time runs out!" Carmen finished, giving the camera a to-die-for smile.

Torean grinned into the camera and said, "Now the time all you athletes have been waiting for, sports.

The Golden Lions Basketball Team suffered a defeat of 69 to 75 during the first game of the season versus the Kensington Raiders. This is not the way we want to start off the season boys, so get it together.

On the plus side, our lady's basketball team won their game against the Raiders 70-55. You go girls!" Torean finished, winking into the camera, "Now let's switch back to Carmen for the lunch menu for today."

"Thanks Tor," Carmen smiled, "For lunch today; you will be having the choice of cheeseburger or cheese pizza, with tater tots, orange slices, and the daily salad bar. If none of this interests you, don't forget you can always buy food from the Wilson Snack Shack."

Then T.I.'s hit song, "Big Thing's Poppin'" came on, and the camera went over to Allen, who was grinning while he danced to the song. "What's good my people of Wilson High? It's time to get it poppin' with the Wilson High Spotlight.

Today the spotlight shines on Bryanna Wilson, grade ten. She has been awarded M.V.P. of the varsity cheer squad for her exceptional leadership skills. Personally, I always love it when people receive awards for wearing barely any clothes, jumping around, and shouting at the top of their lungs. Stuff like this makes my life worth living. You go Bre-Bre!" Allen chuckled, "But in all seriousness, Bryanna Wilson has shone since her freshman year, being a positive leader and role model both in and out of her uniform. No one else deserved this award more than she did."

"Well, that does it with your morning announcements with me, Torean."

"Me, Carmen."

"And ya boy Allen."

"And don't forget, at Wilson High we might tell the news," Torean said.

"But *you* make the news," Carmen finished the sentence, pointing into the camera.

"And that's a wrap!" Allen smiled, and the other two joined him in waving good-bye.

CHARMANE WHITE

The announcements ended with DJ Khaled's "We're Taking Over."

We're taking over, one whole city at a time!

ALLEN RIVERA
Monday, 8:35a.m ~ SOPHOMORE HALLWAY

Rushing to get everything he needed

for his class, Allen hurriedly closed his locker, quietly cursing his alarm clock for not waking him up in time. As he made his way down the long hallway, his nose began to burn from the scent of cinnamon. On any normal occasion, Allen would love to breathe in the smell, but because he heard an increasingly louder *guuuh guuuh ahhh guuuh* along with the aroma, his stomach turned in disapproval for what he knew he was about to encounter.

Allen took every step with caution. If he weren't already so late for class, he would've just taken the long way around to the English classroom. But he didn't have time to waste. Rounding the corner of the sophomore hall, Allen breathed out a sigh of relief; the coast was clear.

"Maybe I was just imagining the whole thing," Allen mumbled to himself as he moved the weight of his books from his left arm to his right. Allen was almost to his class, so he decided to get a drink from the water fountain by the bathroom. With his head bent down, he sipped the cool water, but he couldn't get rid of the cinnamon smell. He crinkled his nose at the odor while he wiped the water off his mouth.

"Ugh!" Allen said, tired of that nasty smell. He felt a heavy weight being placed on his shoulder.

"Whut wrong howney?"

"Aaaah!" Allen screamed in fright. Eyes big in surprise, he gazed up at his stalker, "What do you want Lafonda?" he scowled at her, moving his shoulder out of her reach; a saddened look appeared on her face at the sight of Allen's attitude.

Guuuh guuuh ahhh guuuh

Lafonda stuffed the rest of the Big Texas into her mouth and wiped the excess oils and cinnamon on her lips like it was lip gloss, "*Guuuh*, can't yer boo just stop buy and say hay ta yer?"

Allen looked up at the girl who was two feet taller, a hundred pounds heavier, and at least four years older than he was. Lafonda is bright yellow in complexion, but she had blotches of brown spots on her neck and chest that Allen concluded to be dirt clusters. She wore lavender contacts that made her look like an anime character, and her hair was so nappy and short that she couldn't even put it into a ponytail. Yet somehow, Lafonda managed to tie a rubber band around her scraps. Slicked down with hair gel and bobby pins, Lafonda truly thought she, along with her hairstyle was cute. And on a day like that day, where she had on baby blue lipstick, leggings with decorative rips in them, a half shirt that exposed her flabby stomach with a Hello Kitty belly ring, and a pair of Timberland boots on, she knew that she looked too good for words.

He could not believe that of all the people at Wilson to have a thing for him, it had to be Lafonda Rice.

"Uh Lafonda, I am not your boo," Allen finally managed to say.

"Uh hee-hee, Uh hee-hee!" Lafonda laughed, "Allon, don't bay crayzay boo."

"I have to get to class girl," Allen said to his stalker, attempting to walk past her, but her sticky fingers halted his movement.

"Allon!" Lafonda started.

"Whaaat?" Allen miserably dragged on. He rolled his eyes at her stomach in frustration.

Guuuh guuuh ahhh guuuh

"LAFONDA!" he shouted at her.

Lafonda licked her lips and exposed the sixteen cavities and four brown, decaying teeth that were in her mouth, "I'm sawry boo, but sometimes I get so cawt up in how fine yer aw."

Allen looked at his cell phone and checked the time, "Look, I'm not tryna be rude, but I really need to get to class."

Lafonda took her sticky cinnamon fingers and began to twirl the tiny strand of hair atop her head, "Yer gown lemme get yer numbah before yew go?"

"Yeah, pull out your cell."

As Lafonda started digging around her bra looking for her phone, Allen took his chance to make a run for it. Sprinting to his class, Allen heard Lafonda shout after him, "Awe my boo loves to play hawd to get!"

The bell went off as soon as he reached the classroom door. Entertaining Lafonda's antics, Allen ended up completely missing his first hour class. He was not mad at all that he did not get to go to class; he was insanely nervous about the lecture he knew his mom was going to give him once she found out. Allen checked his surroundings carefully as he walked back to his locker, not wanting another run-in with Lafonda. Though he did catch a whiff of cinnamon, he didn't spot her in the crowd. But knowing Lafonda Rice, she was sure to be around somewhere.

ALLEN RIVERA
Monday, 1:20p.m. ~ SIXTH HOUR

Allen and Patrick sat on the hard wooden stools of home economics reading a paper that gave them directions on how to make fudge brownies.

Patrick scanned the paper again, "Man, we are going to seriously screw these brownies up," he said, shaking his head.

"Whatever Patrick, you already know our greedy butts are gonna eat them."

"Of course!" Patrick agreed, giving Allen a high five.

The two boys walked over to Tiffany and Carmen. The section they shared had a stove, refrigerator, microwave, countertops, and cupboards for a house.

"Hey y'all, what's up?" Tiffany said to the two boys still reading over the cooking instructions.

"Nothin' much," Allen replied, "Just getting ready to burn up these brownies."

Tiffany and Carmen laughed.

"You are so funny Allen!" Carmen told him while she opened up a cabinet to get out the flour.

"Thanks," Allen replied smiling. Patrick nudged him in the side.

"What?" Allen whispered to Patrick.

Patrick rolled his eyes upward, "Don't get all gushy when she gives you a compliment. That is so gay. Really gay."

Allen ignored his comment. Patrick was just a hater.

"Hey, Carmen. I forgot to tell you earlier, but I thought you did a great job on the announcements yesterday," Allen said, looking her dead in her face.

She smiled and Tiffany quieted a laugh.

"Aww thanks, Al. Let's just hope I don't screw up on them today."

"Well, I got your back if you do," Allen smiled, trying to unglue his eyes off of her.

The four of them continued cooking their brownies with a few side conversations. Once the food was done, everyone in the class sat at their tables to eat their brownies.

"Any of y'all goin' to the basketball game on Tuesday?"

Everyone around the table shook their heads.

Tiffany continued, "What about the after party? That's going to be the hottest party of the season!"

"I have to go to work after school," Allen replied. He wasn't really a party person anyway. Being the funny man gave him respect at school, but when he was at a party, it was a different situation.

"What about you Patrick? Football season's over. You can afford to party," Tiffany tried to persuade.

Patrick shook his head, "There's no way I'm tryna get caught at a party where there's alcohol. My mom would kill me!"

Allen looked over at Carmen who didn't seem to be eating anything off her plate. He figured she was probably watching her curvaceous, yet toned figure that was blessed by God himself. So cute, so fine, those curves, that hair…

"What about you Carmen?" Allen asked her.

"Oh, I just have a lot of stuff to do, so I can't go," she took a small bite out of her brownie.

Tiffany rolled her eyes and laughed, "Is that what they're callin' it nowadays?"

Carmen snapped her neck in Tiffany's direction, "Don't start with me Tiff."

"I ain't startin' nothin', but you damn sure know that Im'ma finish it," said Tiffany with her glossy lips turned up and her head rolling with every word she spoke.

"Finish what?" Carmen asked with attitude.

"I'm just sayin'," Tiffany said, folding her arms, "You've been hella busy lately with whichever guy that's got you wrapped around his finger. You must've forgotten that it's T.L.C., not T.L."

Carmen rolled her eyes in exasperation, "Can we talk about this when there aren't *people* around?" Carmen said in a low tone as she moved her eyes in the direction of Allen and Patrick.

"What I look like baby girl? Slavery is over; you don't tell me what to do," Tiffany said rolling her eyes.

"Burn!" Patrick said, laughing at the comment Tiffany made. Tiffany smirked in his direction.

Carmen got defensive, "Tiffany, you must have those micro braids in your head too tight. I can say whatever I wanna say, when I wanna say it. Like you said, it's T.L.C., not that other crap you were talking about."

"*Dayumm*, double burn!" Patrick joked. Allen smacked him upside the head.

"Wha—?" Patrick said, rubbing his head.

Allen ignored his best friend's over exaggerated head rub, instead he focused on the fact that Carmen had picked up her things and left the classroom.

Without thinking, Allen got up, not caring if the teacher would yell at him, and followed Carmen out into the hallway.

"You okay?" Allen said after he grabbed her by the arm to stop her from going any further.

"Yeah, I'm good," Carmen replied, "I just had to get away from Ms. Ghetto Fabulous over there, thinking she runs me."

Allen shrugged his shoulders, "Well, that's Tiffany, she think she the flyest thing since hair weaves."

Carmen laughed, "Allen you are too crazy!"

"That's me, Allen Rivera: The Crazy Mex."

Carmen put her hand on his shoulder like she was preparing to say something to him.

"What yo' fine self doin' out here?"

Carmen removed her hand from Allen's shoulder, and Allen looked over at where the voice was coming from.

Carmen put on her million-dollar smile, "Nothing Keem, just getting some air."

The boy walked up to her with a slight coolness in his stride, and wrapped his arm around her shoulder. Carmen looked over at Allen apologetically. In return, Allen stood silent, bothered by the fact that Carmen smiled harder at Keem than she did at him, yet still hoping that maybe, just *maybe,* her smile was not as sincere as she made it out to be.

"Well, how 'bout I get some air wit' chu?" Keem said, looking Carmen up and down.

"Fine with me," Carmen replied, allowing Keem to lead her away from the home economics classroom, not once looking back at Allen.

Look at him. Allen thought to himself. *With those muscles and that stupid beard. Over there tryna look like T.I. He must think he's so cool, coming up and just taking her away like its just sooo easy. What does he have that I don't? Yeah he got muscles from lifting weights at the juvenile penitentiary, and has money from selling drugs to everyone. And so what if he throws half the junior parties at the school! He's not funny like I am. He doesn't have his own comedy roast on YouTube,* *and do the Wilson High Spotlight like I do. **What?** I just don't get it! He's just a player...Oh yeah, I forgot. He's a player.*

Allen walked back into the classroom, feeling like he lost every bit of progress that he had made.

TOREAN HUDSON
Monday, 1:20p.m. ~ 6TH HOUR

"This frog kinda looks like you, Torean!"
Neisha joked as she prodded the dead frog with her knife.

Neisha, Bryanna, Torean, and Drew all stood around their lab table in biology, dissecting a slimy frog.

"Ooo dawg, she's ova here dissin' you!" Drew laughed.

"Let the ugly hater say what she wants," Torean said smoothly while he stared at Bryanna, who was leaning against the lab table with Torean leaning right over her.

"So like I was sayin' before your hater friend interrupted me," Neisha rolled her eyes and continued cutting open the frog.

"Why didn't you message me back last night?" he finished, looking Bryanna right in the eyes.

Bryanna looked up at Torean, who towered over her, bit her lip, and replied, "I'm sorry, I had to go work out last night. This body does not stay this good without my daily dose of Insanity."

"Well if that was the case, I could've worked you out myself," Torean winked at her, "You know how much I love our work out sessions."

"Ugh! TMI!" Neisha shouted over at the two.

Drew laughed while he continued helping out Neisha with the frog dissection. He was still trying to figure out why he didn't skip school; that frog stuff had him grossed out.

Bryanna slid from under Torean's arms, "I'd like it if you'd keep our business between us, and anyway, it was only *one* time. Nothing worth bragging about."

Torean cocked his head to the side and let out a disbelieving laugh, "So you gon' diss me like that in front of my boy? We both know you liked it, so stop acting like your saddity butt ain't feelin' ya man too, otherwise, you wouldn't have let me hit it in the first place."

Neisha tried to bury her laughter by covering her mouth with her lab jacket sleeve, but even she knew Torean was telling the truth. Ever since that night at Marcus's party, Bryanna and Torean have been playing silly cat and mouse games with each other. First, it started with text messages, then Facebook, then IM, and now Twitter. Bryanna tried to front like she was not feeling Torean and that she didn't fall for every piece of game that came out of his mouth, but Neisha knew she did. And Torean! Torean may have been the biggest man-whore at Wilson, but he had been all up in Bryanna's face every chance he got lately. She didn't understand why they didn't just hook up like all of their friends know they want to.

"Torean, Torean, Torean. When will you learn?" Bryanna teased.

"Learn what?"

"That your stupid games don't work on me!" Bryanna replied, pushing her face closer to his, her teeth glistening with her cocky smile.

"They did that one night," Torean retorted. Drew and he exchanged a dap.

"As you can tell," Neisha interjected. She felt it was time to defend her friend, "It was only *one* night."

"Thank you girl!" Bryanna said, high fiving her friend.

"And as *you* can tell," Drew jumped in, "no one was talkin' to you. Just finish slicing up that stinky frog, and get outta folks business."

Torean shook his head laughing.

"Who do you think you're talking to like that?" Neisha said, rolling her neck and eyes, letting her inner ghetto come out.

"Oh man!" Torean said sarcastically, "Don't make her mad, man or she'll get her country boyfriend on us!" Torean and Drew started acting like they were scared.

Even Neisha had to laugh at what Torean said. She and Trent, her Atlanta-native boyfriend, had been going out for a month at the time, and things had been going great. Not too much drama for her in the boy department.

"So," Bryanna finally said after everyone finished laughing, "Are the Clique Boys going to be at the after-basketball game party on Tuesday?"

Torean looked over at Bryanna and said flirtatiously, "Yeah, especially if your sexy self is gonna be there."

"You already know I'm going to be there," Bryanna said, winking at Torean.

"Well, I'm not coming since Marcus will be there with that skank of his," Neisha said, folding her arms. That skank she was referring to was Lynda Andrews. Marcus dated her after Neisha broke up with him when she found out he only talked to her to win some ignorant sex bet, which he did end up coming out on top with in the end. Even though she had a man and was happy, she still couldn't stand to see those two together. Neisha didn't know why it bothered her so much. It just did.

Drew looked at Neisha and told her, "Girl, Marcus does not want you. Stop being a party pooper and just show up to the party."

"Yeah girl, *please!*" Bryanna begged.

Neisha rolled her eyes. That was her answer.

"Come on! If you don't go, I'll have to hang out with the T.L.C.'s, and you know how thirsty they act," Bryanna begged.

"Baby girl, you don't have to hang out with those chicks when you can chill with your man right here," Torean said, pointing to himself.

"No thank you," Bryanna replied to Torean, completely moving away from him to join her best friend in dissecting the frog.

Drew leaned in close to Torean and whispered, "Yeah, she's sayin' that now, but come the night of the party, she'll be all over you. I guarantee it." A slow grin crept up onto the face of Torean Hudson. Once they were all alone he knew that Bryanna was going to be right in his face, and he couldn't wait for that night to happen.

ALLEN RIVERA
Tuesday, 6:00p.m. ~ Radio Shack

Walking up and down the skinny isles of the Radio Shack, Allen fixed every object that was out of place on the shelves. This particular day was pretty slow, not only at work, but at school too. All day people had been talking about the basketball game that night, and the main circle at Wilson were all hyped up to go to the after party. Even though Allen thought of himself as being in the inner circle, he knew that he wasn't all the way in there. He was funny, but he was no Mike Epps; Allen wasn't officially part of the 'in' crowd.

As the hour passed from six to seven, Allen sat in the chair of the front desk, checking out customers. He couldn't wait to go home and start writing his material for the comedy roast he was going to tape tomorrow night.

A couple minutes after the last customer left, he heard the familiar beep of the opening of the store door, so he looked up to see who it was.

In walked Carmen with her arm interlocked with some Young Jeezy look-a-like. His pants were just about reaching his knees, and his LA fitted cap covered up his eyes. The boy, or man, more like it, looked to be at least in his early twenties.

Talk about not being able to get a girl your own age, thought Allen.

When the thug bit his lower lip while he was checking out Carmen from behind, Allen got a glimpse of the shiny row of diamonds in his teeth.

"Get whatever you want baby," the boy said, "After the way you treated me today, Imma let you spend all my money."

Damn, this dude even sounds like Jeezy! Allen thought as he watched the two walk around the store. He tried to cover his face with a DUB Magazine, so that they didn't notice him staring them down like a hawk. Pretending to read an article on the top Hip-Hop artists of the year, Allen continued to listen to their conversation.

"Aww thanks Derek!" Carmen replied, kissing him on the cheek. Derek pulled her back towards him and kissed her again.

Allen watched as Carmen picked up a tiny camcorder and asked if he would buy it for her.

"Yeah, I'll get it for you sexy. But what you gon' do for me?" the boy asked mischievously.

All Carmen did in response was gave him her award worthy smile.

Allen rolled his eyes and turned the page of his magazine.

He slowly placed his magazine down when the two of them came up to the counter. Carmen gasped and smiled.

"Hey Allen! I didn't know you worked here."

Derek looked from Carmen to Allen, with his eyebrows raised.

Carmen checked out Derek's demeanor and explained, "I go to school with him; we do the announcements together."

"Oh," he said, nodding his head slowly.

"Did you guys find everything okay?" Allen asked the two. He honestly could care less, but it was store procedure and the security cameras were running.

"Yep," they both replied.

Allen took the box containing the camera and rang it up.

"Your total is 209.57," Allen told Derek.

Derek reached into his pocket and slowly pulled out a huge wad of cash. Allen knew he was doing the whole slow motion thing on purpose. After Allen got the money he said, "Have a nice day!" while thinking, *Forget you!"*

The two of them made their way out the store, but not so fast that Allen still heard Derek say, "We are gonna have a good time with this camera."

Oh, what Allen wouldn't have done to be on the other end of that stick? He happened to be a master with cameras too.

But once again, the player won.

ALLEN RIVERA
Wednesday, 7:01p.m. ~ ALLEN'S ROOM

Allen sat in his plush computer chair, and flicked the on switch of his web cam. Once again it was another Wednesday for Allen, and it was time to get to work.

"Wussup, Wussup! It's the Crazy Mex, Allen Rivera, comin' to you from my wonderful bedroom, giving you what you wanna hear. You already know what it is! Roast time!"

Allen slid his chair back some, so that the camera could get a full view of his Spider Man t-shirt and khaki shorts, and continued, " Now, I've talked about many people like Lil Wayne and his nappy dreads, Drake always crying over a girl, and Trey Songz shouting out phrases like he has turrets. But today, I just have to get this one thing off my chest. Let me start by playing a song."

Allen pressed the play button on his media player.
Lil' mama so hood, (I love your girl)
Lil' mama stay fly, (I love your girl)
Wife beater with the denim, (I love your girl)
She keeps them heels on high, (I love your girl)
Man look at shorty roll, (I love your girl)
Man look at shorty go, (I love your girl)
(I'm sorry I gotta be up on your wild girlfriend.)

CHARMANE WHITE

After he pressed the stop button, he closed his eyes as if he was in remorse and said, "Yes people, today I will be roasting The Dream.

Now we all know that he makes so hot songs like "Bed", "Shawty is a Ten", and "Falsetto", but that doesn't mean he can sing them. This man thinks that just because Ne-Yo goes from writing songs to singing hits that he can too, but if y'all haven't noticed, Ne-Yo actually knows how to sing. I mean, if this is the case, then no one needs to have any talent; all we have to do is write a bomb song and put some auto tune or somethin' over it and then we got ourselves a hit record.

I mean, nothing about The Dream says star. He can't sing, he's ugly, and he dresses like Kanye West on crack. Leather pants are not your thing man. And then on top of that, he had the nerves to hook up with Christina Milian. For a short while there, we had two people who couldn't hit a note. Thank goodness that Christina grew some brains and left him while she still had some vocal chords. I heard their baby came out sounding like T-Pain without the auto tune. The main question that I'm left to ponder with, and hopefully others feel me on this is why would some idiot give this prick a record deal when he can't even sing? This is ridiculous!"

Allen pounded his fists on the desk in over aggravation, "You know what? I can't do this anymore. It's time for me to go in on his ass! Get yo' big I eat cookies 'cuz they make me happy lookin' butt. Yo' big Pillsbury Dough Boy lookin' boy! Skinny jeans are only for skinny people Dream, get it through your head! Look at yo' big walkin' on the moon lookin' boy! Man, look at The Dream for a quick second. Don't he look like his breath stank? Big stanky dude! Try and sweat that fat off!"

Allen finally got done ribbin' at the Dream, "Aight, aight, now like I said before, he makes hot songs, but man, he does

PLAYER *40* HATER

not have the voice to match. This is a sad, sad day in the world of R&B. First Cassie, and now this guy?

When will the madness stop?"

Allen shook his head and then looked back up into the camera and said, acting like he was depressed, "That's it for tonight. And don't forget if you want me to roast one of your favorite celebs, e-mail me who you want me to roast and I'll see what I can do.

Once again, it's the Crazy Mex, Allen Rivera comin' to you live from my dirty room. I'll see you next Wednesday. I'm out of here!"

Allen let the rest of Dream's song play, singing, "Radio killa, we beat the track up like guerillas!", before he cut off his web cam.

He found the media file of his roast and uploaded it to YouTube.

Now it was time for the world to check it out.

ALLEN RIVERA & TOREAN HUDSON
Thursday, 10:22a.m. ~ SPANISH II

The kids settled in their seats waiting for Mr. Brunning to get to class. Allen sat there with a smug look on his face because everyone in the classroom was giving him his props for the roast he did last night on YouTube. Even Carmen came up to him and told him that she checked it out. That was mostly why he was walking around acting like he was a god.

"Hey class," Brunning said while he put all his things away, getting ready to start class, "today we will be learning about the history of Spain and where they get their customs from."

All the kids groaned.

"This man must be crazy thinking I'm going to sit here and listen to this," Torean said to Allen who was sitting right beside him.

"I feel you bro," Allen agreed, nodding his head. It wasn't like he could really concentrate on what they were learning today anyways because he was too busy staring at the back of Carmen's head.

"You gettin' a good view?" Torean joked, checking out Allen stare at Carmen.

"What are you talking about?" Allen replied, taking his eyes off the gorgeous girl and onto Torean.

Torean huffed and said to Allen, "I think I would know if a guy is feeling a girl, especially when that guy knows that he has no chance in hell at getting with her."

"Since we both know that I don't have any chance at getting at her," Allen said with attitude in his voice, "why would you think I'd waste my time looking at her? We're just friends."

"Dude, I was just playing. Calm down. And anyway, *she* might think you're just friends, but *you* want it to be something more. I don't blame you; she's fine."

Allen shook his head, "I'm not her type."

"Are the two of you talking about anything important Mr. Rivera?" Mr. Brunning shouted to the back of the room at Torean and Allen. Everyone turned around at the two to see what was going on.

"Yeah we're talking about something important, so how about you turn your fat face around and teach the rest of these kids," Allen shouted right back at the teacher. All the kids started laughing.

Mr. Brunning got red in the face, but turned around and finished teaching the subject just like Allen told him to do, too afraid to retort back because he didn't want another roasting session to happen again.

Allen and Torean continued with their conversation.

"You don't know if you're not her type."

Allen laughed at Torean's stupidity, "If I was her type, she wouldn't have dissed me to hang out with some T.I. look-a-like guy a couple of days ago," Allen's tan face flushed red when he thought back on how bad he felt when Carmen did that to him.

Torean slightly grinned, "You're getting really emotional for someone who's supposedly not interested in her."

"Man, no one's getting emotional. I'm just stating the facts, and the fact is that she wouldn't go for someone like me."

While they were talking, Carmen turned around and smiled in their direction. Allen returned the smile, though his was a bit weaker because Carmen took him off guard with her dazzling gesture. Rolling her eyes in Brunning's direction, Carmen clearly signaled that she couldn't stand this class as much as the next Spanish speaking kid.

Once Carmen turned back around, Allen looked back at Torean and said, "Man, who am I kidding? You and I both know I want her."

Torean looked at Allen and shrugged his shoulders, "What's stopping you from getting at her?" Torean didn't understand what Allen was stressing about. Maybe it was because he never had a problem with getting whatever he wanted when he wanted it, and that he was one of the most popular and good-looking guys in his grade. But in Torean's opinion, which really did matter at the school, Allen wasn't ugly and he was really funny, so Torean didn't get what the big problem was.

"What's stopping me from getting her?" Allen restated.

"Guys like *you* are stopping me from getting her."

"What?" Torean said taken aback.

Allen answered, "Guys like you. You know, cool, good-looking, dress to impress, party-going players. You're a player Torean, and those are the type of guys Carmen goes for, not the funny guys who would actually treat her with respect. She wants a player."

Torean leaned back in his seat and turned his head towards Allen. While slowly rubbing his hand over his chin, he replied, "Then that's what we'll do; I'm gonna make you a player."

Allen looked skeptically at Torean, began to gaze at Carmen thoughtfully, and turned his attention back to the famous Torean Hudson once again.

"I'm in."

ALLEN RIVERA
Saturday, 9:30a.m ~ HOME/ HALLOWAY
APARTMENTS

Allen hopped down his wooden staircase leading to the main part of the house, dressed in a simple white T-shirt and khaki shorts and ran into the kitchen where he was greeted by a plate of sausages, bacon, pancakes and orange juice, and a surprised mother standing by the stove.

"Hijo! What are you doing running around like a psycho?" Rosalie shouted, holding her hand to her chest.

"Sorry ma gotta go!" Allen said hurriedly, stuffing as much food as he could into his mouth.

Allen's mom put her pancake batter-covered hands on her apron-clad hips and said, "And where do you have to go?"

He quickly replied, "I'm meeting up with friends," Allen grabbed his coat, his car keys, and his cell phone, and booked it out the door. He did not want to be late.

The speedometer read 70mph's, but no cops were around, so Allen just kept on speeding through the 40mph intersections. He ignored the frequent horn honks and a few shouts from other drivers. Allen needed to be at Torean's house by ten o'clock, and it was already nine-fifty. His alarm clock really had something against him; it was never waking him up on time lately.

Allen drove through Halloway Apartments. They were all red brick with silver accents on the windows, doors, and garages. There were huge trees on every lawn and a community park in the center of the apartment complex. It was weird for Allen to picture Torean living in a place like this. It looked too innocent for a person like Torean Hudson.

Once he found the right apartment address, he hopped out of the Chevy and ran up the short steps to press the buzzer.

"Who is it?" Torean's voice blared through the speakers.

"Al," he answered out of breath.

What he got in response was a buzz letting him in.

Allen ran up three flights of stairs until he got to a door labeled #4. He knocked three times before Torean opened the door.

The two of them gave each other a play while they exchanged their greetings. Torean lead Allen inside his house where more people greeted him.

Allen should have known that the Clique Boys would be there; it was very rare to see them hanging without one another.

"What's up?" Allen said to the three swagged out looking guys, thinking to himself that he'd soon be just like them.

Marcus, Drew, and Ricky all gave Allen a play, secretly wondering why Torean invited him over.

Allen noticed how all the Clique Boys looked so…wantable. They were all sitting on the long black sofa like they were not interested in anything around them. It kind of seemed like they practiced looking uninterested, because they were pulling it off so well. They were dressed to impress even though they were probably going to be staying over Torean's house all day. And on top of that, all four of the guys' cell phones had been going off, but not one of them looked to see who called or texted. The Clique Boys must have been used to being called from random women in the middle of the day. If Allen hadn't known them better, he'd say that they were getting ready to pose for a layout in VIBE; they just looked that cool.

Torean stood by Allen and said, "I called all you guys over here because I need your help with something."

The Clique Boys looked at each other in curiosity.

Torean put his hand on Allen's shoulder, "Allen here, for reasons that none of you guys need to worry about, wants to be made into a player."

The Clique Boys burst out laughing. Allen uncomfortably switched the weight on his feet while scratching his head awkwardly. He was used to making people laugh, but never had he been a fan of being the joke.

"I'm sorry man, can you repeat that one more time?" Ricky said to Torean, still laughing.

Allen stepped forward and answered, "I want to become a player."

"And all of us are gonna do whatever it takes for him to become one," Torean told them, looking around to see if anyone thought other than what he said. They all looked like they were on board. Skeptical, but on board nonetheless.

"So this is how we're going to do this," Torean looked over at Marcus, "I want you to show this dude how to dress. There's no way he's gonna get girls walkin' around Wilson in the clothes that he wears."

"What's wrong with my clothes?" Allen asked, looking down at his outfit.

Marcus replied, "Well first off, you're wearing shorts during winter—"

"It's only the beginning of November!"

"— and you're wearing black Nikes with a white shirt. You are going to need all the help that you can get," Marcus finished looking him up and down like this was going to be a huge challenge.

"Drew," Torean continued, "You're in charge of making sure that this boy gets to know everybody who's anybody at Wilson and other schools that we hang with. I'm talkin' about girls, ball players, party throwers, drug hook-ups, and of course all the players that we know."

Drew nodded his head and took out his cell phone, looking for the phone numbers of people that Allen needed to get connected with.

"Torean, I don't do drugs," Allen said.

Everyone ignored his comment and Torean continued on, "And Ricky, I need you to teach this boy how to talk like us. There's no wonder this boy can't get a girl; he talks like such a lame sometimes," Torean jokingly smiled at Allen before he turned back to Ricky, "Just show him how it's supposed to be done."

"I got chu," Ricky replied.

Once Torean was done giving all his friends instructions, he turned to Allen and told him, "Come with me, I'm gonna teach you the main things you need to know about becoming a player."

"What's that?" Allen asked intriguingly.

"The most important rules every man should know," Torean reached into his designer pockets and pulled out a folded piece of loose-leaf paper. He handed the paper to Allen as if it was a lost passage in the Bible.

Biting the inside of his cheek in apprehension, Allen took the paper from Torean and opened it up. In big, bolded letters, the heading of the paper read TOREAN HUDSON'S RULES ON HOW TO BECAOME A PLAYER. Allen dryly laughed at what he saw, but when he looked over at Torean who was watching him intensely, he got serious again and began to read the rules.

"Rule number one: dress to impress every day," said Allen,

"Well thanks to Marcus that should not be a problem," he said more to himself than to Torean.

"Rule two: make sure the breath is on point," he laughed at the rest of the rule, "Gum only cost one dollar."

"Rule three: talk with the eyes, not with the mouth," Allen squinted his eyes at the paper, "What in the world does this mean Torean?"

Torean lightly chuckled, "The rules are very simple, Allen. Talkin' with the eyes and not the mouth simply means that before you waste your time verbally communicating with a girl, you should instead scope her out with your eyes. You always want to make sure the girl is worth talking to before you run game on her."

"Uhh?"

"Alright, check this: say I see a bad ass female and I want to go holler at her. I'm gonna check her out *with my eyes* to see if her body language in on the same page as mine, which it usually is, and once I see that she's feelin' me too, then I'll go in with my game," Torean put his hand on Allen's shoulder, "Does it make sense to you now?"

"Yeah, yeah," replied Allen, "Rule four says that when you *do* speak to a girl, act like she's lucky to be talking to you, not like you're lucky to be talking to her."

"Right. Seriously, even if Megan Good is having a conversation with you, you better make sure you never show how thirsty you are," Torean added in.

Allen laughed, "Okay, okay. Next rule: Pick-up lines are a must, but don't get them off the internet," Allen scratched his head while he asked Torean, "Can I get an example?"

"Things like 'I hope there's a fireman around, 'cause you're smokin'" will definitely not get you too far with the ladies."

Looking let down, Allen replied, "So basically, everything I've been saying to girls can *never* be used again?"

"Now you're getting it."

"Rule six," continued Allen, "Learn how to touch a girl in all the right places. One bad mistake and you're going to get a slap in the face."

"What do you consider a 'bad mistake'?" Allen asked Torean, using air quotes.

Torean answered, "Don't go grabbing a girl's butt ten minutes into meeting her. You're a player, not a perv—remember that."

"Gotcha," Allen replied, "Okay, rule number seven: If you make a girl mad, sweet talk your way out of it. Excuses, excuses, excuses," Allen slowly nodded his head, "I actually understand this one.

"Rule eight: don't juggle what you can't handle."

"Yeah," Torean said, "handling girls can be very messy. You never want to get involved with two girls who are in the same class, or girls who hang in the same social group—that causes too much gossip and drama."

"Nine: make the girl feel like she's the sexiest thing in the world," Allen looked at Torean like he was stupid, "Well *duh*!"

"Shut up and finish reading the rules Al."

"Rule ten: never brag to your boys about who you're about to hook up with because they will try to steal her from you."

"Rule eleven: run game until you can't run game anymore."

"Rule twelve: treat your girl so good that she brags about you to her friends, because then her friends will want to see what you're really about," said Allen.

"If you know what I mean," Torean mischievously laughed.

"Whatever," Allen laughed as well, "Anyway, rule thirteen says to pay for everything on the first date, but after that she better cough up some cash," Allen nodded his head in approval, "This has to be my favorite rule so far."

Well keep reading," Torean said, "They only get better from here."

"Rule fourteen: never give a girl your home phone number. Cell phone *only*? But why?"

Torean began to explain, "You always want to limit the communication sources that you share with a female. The more ways they can get in contact with you means that there are more ways they can snoop around and get you caught up."

"I get it," Allen continued, "Rule fifteen: If there's a hot party, there are even hotter girls, so make sure you go to all of them."

"Sixteen: Don't forget, you can't be a player unless you have the face."

"At the end of the day, girls want hot guys, plain and simple," Torean told Allen, "And by the time we're done with you, you will definitely be that type of guy girls want."

"Rule number seventeen—man these are a lot of rules—try not to holler at too many ugly girls; doing so will ruin your rep."

"Eighteen: *but* you should only get at ugly girls if they have something you want."

Torean clearly saw that Allen was confused, so before he could ask his thousandth question, Torean told him, "If there is an ugly girl stalking the halls of Wilson, willing to trick off her money on you, then show her a good time. And when I say 'good time', I mean be nice to her—I better not catch you holding her hand or blowin' up her Twitter feed."

"That's kind of rude isn't it?" Allen asked.

"Look, she's the one who offered to be used; you just took her up on her offer."

Allen shook his head, "Rule nineteen: don't ever catch feelings for the girl first."

"And last but not least, rule number twenty: a player never stops being a player," Allen finished reading the rules and handed the loose-leaf paper back to Torean.

Torean re-pocketed the paper and said to Allen, "Now let's go put these rules into action."

"Let's do it."

THE NEW IMPROVED ALLEN RIVERA
Monday, 7:45a.m. ~ PARKING LOT

Allen smoothly got out of his truck, and his friend Patrick greeted him. Allen stood by his car, leaned up against it like he was an A&F model. He pulled out his cell phone and stared down at it like he was bored at whatever was going on around him and said, "What's good Patrick?"

Patrick glared at Allen like he was just seeing him for the very first time; it was sort of like he was. Allen cut his curls off and now rocked a simple low cut. He wore dark washed jeans with fashionable rips in them, a charcoal heather- gray scoop-neck under a thick tan polo cardigan with the dark gray logo, and on his feet was a simple, yet fashionable pair of tan Polo boots. Allen had two diamond studs in his ears and he smelled just like I AM KING cologne. Patrick watched Allen, wondering what in the world was going on with his best friend.

"What has gotten into you?" Patrick finally asked.

Allen looked down at himself and replied smoothly, "I just decided to switch my style up a bit, know what I'm sayin'?"

Patrick squinted his eyes at Allen, hoping that if he stared at him long enough he would figure out why he was acting and looking so strange, "No, I don't know what you're sayin'."

"You know, I gotta do what I gotta do. Man, you know I gotta stay fly and keep it pimpin'."

Patrick stood there with his mouth wide open in shock.

"What the heck are you saying?"

Allen laughed and rubbed his hand over his chin suavely and said, "It's the new me. I kinda like it."

"Are you on drugs?"

"Naw fam, I just wanna keep it real and do what it do, you know what I mean?"

Patrick shook his head in disbelief and the two of them began walking into the school. Everyone around them was looking at Allen, wondering why he looked so different. The stylish clothes and confident swagger that oozed off Allen had the teenage boys of Wilson High worried about their new competition. The girls, on the other hand, could care less about why Allen looked so cool. All that mattered to them was that he looked good and had the attitude to match. As he walked past the ladies, they were all checking out the certified cutie. Patrick gawked at all the buck-eyed staring going on; it was like he was in the Twilight Zone. Allen Rivera simply took it all in, pretending like he was not beyond excited that all eyes were on him. Caught up in his ego trip, Allen unknowingly sauntered past Lafonda Rice, and she just about lost her mind.

"Oh my gawd!" Lafonda shouted in surprise. She leaned her heavy weight against a nearby wall to steady herself. *Guuuh*, "My baybay! Look at my baybay!" *ahhh guuuh*.

"Everyone's staring at you," Patrick whispered to Allen while they walked down the sophomore hallway.

Allen put his hands in his designer pockets and continued walking like he was in no hurry to go anywhere and replied, "That's 'cause they feelin' me."

"You must be on drugs Allen! Why are you acting like this?" to Patrick, the new Allen sounded ignorant, cocky, and high; not the type of friend he wanted to be around. For whatever reason Allen was acting like that, Patrick was curious to know why.

While the two of them were walking, Allen was trying to remember what the Clique Boys taught him about checking out girls. *That's right, I have to glance their way and look them up and down like I'm picturing them naked.*

Allen spotted the four boys standing by their lockers surrounded by beautiful women; that was exactly where he needed to be.

"Aye Patrick, lemme get at chu a lil' bit later, aight?" Allen said, not even giving Patrick enough time to answer before he walked slowly and smoothly towards the Clique Boys' lockers.

Patrick rolled his eyes. Now he knew why Allen was acting like this. Patrick was pissed that his best friend dissed him because the Clique Boys found some odd type of interest in him for some reason. He hoped that Allen would get back to his senses, and very soon, for the sake of their friendship.

"Well, well, well, if it isn't our little project," Torean said, his voice quiet in subtle disinterest, but loud enough for all the Clique Boys to hear, when he saw Allen walking towards them.

"What's good?" Allen said to the four boys, giving them all a dap. While he was giving one to Drew, he practiced the "undressing with the eyes" thing on the sexy freshman who was on his hip. The girl looked up at Allen and gave him a flirtatious smile.

All the boys noticed it and Torean said, "How you been holdin' up?"

"I'm aight, just chillin'."

"I mean with the girls," Torean said.

Allen cleared his throat and confidently tried to reply, "I haven't really seen too many fly females, but when I do, Imma get at 'em. You already know."

The Clique Boys all looked at one another and smirked.

Torean spoke, "Now, you may look the part right now, but if you can't act the part, this isn't going to work."

"Yeah man, show us what you can do," Marcus said to Allen, smiling mischievously in Torean's direction.

Allen got nervous, "What y'all want me to do?"

"You see that mixed girl standing by Kayla?"

Allen looked across the hallway where Kayla was standing with her friends, "Who? Victoria?"

"Yeah her," Torean replied nodding his head slowly.

Allen's palms started to get sweaty, "What about her?"

Ricky chimed in, "Ask her out on a date."

Allen laughed at their obvious joke, "You really want me to ask a Varsity Cheerleader out on a date? You guys are too funny!" He knew that when he undertook this change that he would have to be a ladies' man, but Allen did not really think that he would actually have to do anything. Looking the part was one thing, but actually putting his game face on and getting down to business was a whole other story. A whole other, *scarier* story.

Torean looked at Allen and said, "Who said we were joking? Now go over there and put your lessons to work."

"Whatever man," Allen said. He put his hands back in his pockets and slowly made his way across the hall where Victoria was standing.

"Hey Kayla, what's up?" while he asked Kayla what was up, he smoothly moved his eyes up and down Victoria's body and bit his lip flirtatiously. Victoria noticed what he was doing and moved around nervously.

"I'm okay? And you?" Kayla replied.

"I would be okay, if your gorgeous friend here would go out on a date with me."

Kayla laughed and looked around at her friends who were all looking at Allen, hoping that he was talking about one of them, and asked, "Who?"

"You right there ma, with those skinny jeans lookin' like they're painted on."

All the girls giggled in Victoria's direction and she smiled at Allen.

"Can I talk to you in private for a second?" he asked.

"Sure," Victoria said, grinning curiously at Allen.

Allen led her a couple of feet away from where her friends were standing, so that the Boys could see him run game.

"Yeah shawty, I was checkin' you out and I just wanna get to know you," Allen said coolly.

Victoria asked him, "So what do you want to do?"

"You really wanna know the answer to that?" Allen asked, looking at Victoria mischievously.

Victoria laughed and replied, "Just call me when you ready to have a good time."

Allen pulled his phone out of his pocket and handed it to Victoria so that she could put her number in his phone. This was the first girl's phone number he had ever gotten, and though he was chill and nonchalant on the outside, in the inside he was fist pumping in the ultimate celebration.

"I got you sexy, Imma call you soon," he said while locking his phone.

"You better," Victoria said flirtatiously, winking in his direction before she made her way back over to her friends who were looking at her enviously, jealous that Allen approached Victoria instead of one of them.

Allen smiled to himself and turned around to go back by the Clique Boys. While he was walking, he turned his head down the hallway where he noticed Carmen staring at him. He gave her a short head nod, but to his surprise, when she noticed that he was looking back at her, she roughly turned her head with her face scrunched up unattractively, sending clear signals to Allen that she was mad at him for something. Still looking sour, Carmen attempted to start up a conversation with the rest of her girls, but they were all too busy still checking out the new and improved Allen Rivera to really care about what she had to say.

Allen walked back towards the Clique Boys' lockers, his practiced chill demeanor replaced with a slight furrow in his thick brows from wondering what Carmen could possibly be mad at him about.

TOREAN HUDSON
Monday, 11:20a.m. ~ LUNCH

Torean stood up from his lunch table

filled with gorgeous boys and disgusting food, and casually strolled over to the table where the "Queen B's", aka Bryanna and Neisha sat.

"Hey Bre, what's up?" Torean asked, flirtatiously rubbing his hand on her lower back while she sat there eating an apple.

Bryanna and the rest of her friends looked up at Torean, "Why are you touching me like you know me?" Bryanna said rolling her eyes in annoyance, Torean laughed, "That's only because you won't let me get to know you."

"Whatever you say Torean."

Torean sat on the empty chair at the table and looked over at Neisha who was sitting close up on her boyfriend Trent. He looked back at Bryanna and whispered, "Why can't you let me do those things to you?"

"Because you're a whore Torean."

Everyone at the table started laughing, including Torean. He placed his hand over his heart and said romantically, "I'm willing to change my ways if you'd let a brutha get some play."

"And what exactly does 'get some play' mean to you?" Neisha interjected.

Torean rolled his eyes. She was lucky her boyfriend was sitting there or he would have said something to piss her off.

"I just wanna hang with you. I don't want to only get to be with you when you're tipsy or anything like that, if you know what I mean," Torean answered to Bryanna.

Bryanna put her hand on top of Torean's and said, "Tor, there are so many girls around here that you can try to manipulate, so why are you trying to waste your time talking to me when you obviously know how hard I am to get?"

Torean gave Bryanna one of his famous smiles, bored his grey eyes into her brown ones, and said, "Maybe that's because I like a challenge. You ever think of that?"

Bryanna nervously looked down at her barely eaten food and Torean smiled at her obviously being bothered by what he said to her. He smoothly stood up from the table and gave Trent a play before he said, "Alright then, Imma go."

He turned to leave and then quickly turned back to the table and said, "The Clique Boys are throwing a party on Friday and all of you guys are invited," he placed his caramel hand on Bryanna's shoulder and said, "Especially you."

Bryanna turned her head away from Torean so that he could not see her blush. She had to give him his props; he definitely knew how to run game. Bryanna just had to make sure that she didn't let him win too many rounds or she might just find herself getting hurt.

CARMEN SANCHEZ
Wednesday, 2:10p.m ~ GIRL'S BATHROOM

The T.L.C. s all stood around the huge
mirror in the girl's restroom fixing their makeup, their hair,
and their outfits. It was the passing time before the last class of
the day, so no one was really in a rush to get to class, except
for Carmen because she had to do the student announcements.

Shaniquia, Lynda, and the rest of their friends were leaned
against the tiled wall talking about the latest news to hit
Wilson High.

"Yeah girl, I heard he's going out on a date with Victoria,"
Lynda said, scratching her weave.

"I know girl. Allen has definitely turned into a certified
sexy, and on top of that, he's been hanging around the Clique
Boys too. You already know that if the Clique Boys wanna
hang out with him then he has to be hot," Shaniquia added.

Tiffany turned around and faced the girls so that she could
include herself in the conversation, "Doesn't it seem like he
became a total ten overnight? I mean one day he's cracking
jokes and never matching his clothes, and the next day he has
swagger, he's dressing to impress, haircut, voice smooth, and
getting play from some of the coolest sophomores at our
school. I don't know what made Allen change, but I might
have to test him out," Shaniquia and Tiffany gave each other a
high five and laughed at Tiffany's joke. Carmen rolled her
eyes while she was applying her eye shadow and said, "So

does this mean that every girl at our school has a thing for Al now because he's so cool?"

Lynda nodded her head.

Shaniquia rolled her eyes at Lynda and said, "Girl, shut up. You already got yourself a man. A Clique Boy at that."

Lynda did exactly what Shaniquia told her to do, and shut right up.

Lauren finally stopped staring at herself in the mirror long enough to add in, "I think I might try to get Allen's attention so that he'll ask me out on a date too. What's the point of being a T.L.C. if we can't have the best of the best?"

"And you think Allen is the best?" Carmen asked, putting her eye shadow away and folding her arms across her chest.

"Well he'll be the best after he gets through with me," Lauren said seductively, biting her lip and winking.

Carmen rolled her eyes, "You guys are such sluts. What makes you think that Allen even wants you? If you haven't noticed, he hasn't spoken to any of us, so do you think that maybe he isn't interested?"

Tiffany smiled, "Oh, I know what this is about. You're just pissed because now that Allen's popularity is going up, he won't be slobbering all over you anymore, right?"

"Tiffany, it has nothing to do with that!"

"Boo-boo, I think it does. You need to back your Spanish self off his wood." Tiffany bitchily replied, smirking.

Carmen picked up her things, walked out of the bathroom, and headed into the direction of the media room. Messing with them, she ended up being a few minutes late for announcements, and she really wasn't in the mood to hear Kayla snap at her. She definitely wasn't in the mood to see the new and improved Allen Rivera get flirted with by every girl in the room either. Carmen just did not understand why she was getting so angry at the sight and mention of how cute and swagged out Allen was. It was not like she couldn't have any guy she wanted, but did that mean that she wanted Allen now too?

As she walked down the hallway, she could clearly hear that the rest of the girls had made their way out of the bathroom and were on their way to class. Trying to keep her distance from them, she heard Tiffany say, "Don't hate the player baby; hate the game."

Carmen rolled her eyes. Typical Tiffany Rodgers; always talking mess, yet always speaking the truth. Carmen was hating and she knew it, but there was absolutely nothing she could do to stop herself from worrying about other girls being interested in Allen Rivera.

ALLEN RIVERA
Friday, 8:00p.m. ~ PARTY

The past week had been amazing for Allen. He made so many new friends who just wanted to hang around him because of Torean. The girls were all on his jock that week too. Once word got around that Allen Rivera was going on a date with Victoria, every girl at Wilson gave him the eye, and even a few hollers.

Allen practically spent all his money on new clothes, his parents thought he had done all this to be rebellious, and he practically lost his best friend because he had been hanging with the Clique Boys so much, but to Allen, everything was worth it. There he was at a party on a Friday night. Beautiful women and good music; he couldn't think of any other place that he'd rather want to be.

Allen noticed Drew opening the front door, allowing three sexy, gorgeous, and fine ladies to walk inside.

Standing on the wall, Allen straightened himself up and pulled out his cell phone, acting as if he didn't notice the T.L.C.'s walk into the room.

Tiffany and her girls were all wearing various shades of blue in their outfits. Tiffany rocked a navy and white, striped long sleeve t-shirt with faded skinny jeans and tan UGG's on her feet. Lauren had on a blue jean skirt and a light-blue tank top, and silver flats, with a light-blue bow on top. And Carmen was wearing a simple white v-neck shirt with a blue scarf tied around her neck, ripped skinny jeans, and white mini UGG boots.

All the girls were immediately greeted by all the single boys at the party. They definitely knew how to get the boys' attention. Allen rolled his eyes in their direction. He wasn't mad that the boys were in his "girl's" face, but he was mad about the fact that she was grinning right back in theirs.

Allen noticed that ever since he started acting like a player, Carmen had been acting funny around him. Like when they were in Spanish class the first day he changed, she didn't speak to him when she walked in. She just glared at him and talked to Torean. Then when Carmen, Patrick, Tiffany, and he all had to cook chicken a la king in home economics, she spoke to everyone else except him, and when Allen would say something to her, she would just give him one word answers. And not to mention how earlier that day when they were filming the announcements, they had to re-film the scene where Carmen introduced Allen for the Wilson High Spotlight because every time she said his name she would say it like it was some sort of curse word. Allen couldn't figure out why she was acting so bitchy with him. It wasn't like he flirted with girls whenever she was around, even though it seemed like Carmen was always there on the scene when Allen was trying to get some play from the ladies. It just didn't make sense to him why she hated him all of a sudden.

Torean and Marcus came up to Allen, who was still acting like he was texting someone on his cell phone, and Torean said, "Al, you do know this is a party, right?"

Huffing, Allen replied, "Yeah man, I'm not stupid."

"Then get off the phone and do what you're supposed to do."

Being a player is harder than it looks. Allen thought as he got himself off the wall and began to search for any easy targets. He spotted a senior girl with a really pretty face and thick hips, who was sitting at a wooden table with a small group of her friends. Allen casually walked past the table, but not before staring at the girl long enough to get her attention, and then went to stand by the staircase railing on the other side of the room. Allen noticed that the girl was checking him out, so he gave her the head nod, telling her to come over by him. The senior got up from her table and went over to Allen and he grabbed her by the wrist, "Hey ma, I saw your sexy self sittin' over there, so I had to get at you," Allen checked out her caramel skin, short curly hair, and her nice sized butt.

"Oh really?" the girl asked smiling curiously.

Allen nodded his head slowly, checking her out, top to bottom, "Yeah, really. So what's yo' name, sexy?"

"Mariah."

"Oh, that's a hot name. I like it."

Mariah bit her lip flirtatiously and said, "Well, I'm a hot girl."

"Hell yeah you are," Allen replied, not once getting excited that he was running game on a senior; the rules told him that she was supposed to be the one getting happy.

Allen continued, "So what you plannin' on doin' tonight?"

She shrugged her shoulders, "Nothing. Probably just hang out and get drunk."

"Fo' sho', fo' sho' shawty. I feel you."

Mariah leaned in closer to Allen and whispered, "If you get bored tonight, just holler at me, and I'll do whatever I can to keep you occupied."

Allen raised his eyebrows and asked, "And what do you have in mind?"

She leaned back into his ear and began to tell him all the things she knew he wanted to hear. While Allen was getting sweet nothings whispered in his ear, he spotted Carmen checking out the whole situation, and when she saw that he had noticed her, she began to make her way towards him. She walked confidently over towards Allen, her long glossy hair catching every bit of wind that came in contact with her.

Allen didn't move or fidget when he saw Carmen coming his way; he just stood there, letting Mariah continue on with speaking dirty to him.

"Sorry, I didn't mean to interrupt your *thing*," Carmen said to Allen when she came up by him. Mariah slowly moved her mouth away from his ear, but not before kissing him on the cheek, "Too bad you did."

Carmen rolled her eyes and Allen smirked. Mariah told Allen, "Don't forget what I told you," before slowly, but seductively walking back towards her friends.

Allen touched his cheek, "You know I won't, sexy."

Carmen's eyes got big because she couldn't believe he was doing this right in front of her. Allen pulled his cell phone back out, "What's up C?"

Carmen smiled in disbelief, "Nothing. I just wanted to break up the freak fest that was going on here. Everyone was looking at that skank slobbering all over you."

"Naw ma, she wasn't slobbin' on me," he chuckled, "Not yet anyway."

"Ooo! Allen's such a big time player now, isn't he?" Carmen said sarcastically.

"So now you can speak to me? Only when there's a girl in my face?"

"You're getting a little bit too rude now, aren't you Allen?"

"I just call it how I see it," Allen replied, putting his cell phone back in his pocket.

Carmen placed her hands on her hips, "And how exactly do you see it Allen? You're the one that started to change overnight."

"And you're the only one who doesn't seem to like it."

"I never said I didn't like it."

"Well how else am I supposed to take it when all of a sudden you start treating me like I'm dirt? We were supposed to be friends, and you started bitchin' me out every time I came around you."

Carmen lowered her voice, "That's not true Allen. I only started bitching you out when I saw you talking to those wanna-be skanks at school."

Allen raised his eyebrows in disbelief. Now everything started to match up with him. He finally figured out why Carmen acted that way. Allen didn't want to look stupid and ruin his new found rep if he said this, but he just had to find out.

"You like me, don't you?"

Carmen rolled her eyes and smiled at the same time.

"Don't you?" Allen said again, this time more like the way Torean would say it to a girl.

"Carmen doesn't like guys; guys like Carmen," she said back to him, crossing her arms.

"Is that right?"

"Yeah, it is."

Allen looked her up and down, "Well, I'm feelin' you, so hopefully you feelin' ya boy too."

"You might be a player now Allen, but that doesn't stop me from thinking that everything you say is a joke."

"I'm not tryna be funny, ma. I'm keepin' it real wit' chu."

Carmen gave him her famous eye roll, "How about you keep it real with me and dance with me to this song."

Allen shook his head and laughed, "I do not dance."

"The player doesn't know how to get it on the floor?"

"I can get it in somewhere else," he said mischievously.

Carmen ignored his comment, "C'mon, all you have to do is stand there and let me do all the work."

"Fine, I'll let you work me, but next time, I get to put work down on you," Allen told her, while the two of them walked by the dance area.

Carmen shook her head and smiled, "I'm gonna kick Torean's butt for teaching you this stuff."

"What makes you think Torean taught me anything?"

"Because, this is some of the bull that only Torean Hudson would say to me."

The speakers were blaring "Practice" by Drake and all the girls were trying to get on the floor to dance to the popular song. Carmen turned around so that her butt was bumping against Allen's groin while she rocked her thick hips to the beat. Allen just stood there, not really knowing what to do. He saw how the other guys were grabbing their girl's waists and pulling them in closer, so Allen mimicked what they did. Carmen smiled at him and began to dance even sluttier. Torean was sitting on the couch with the Clique Boys and saw how Allen was working Carmen. They all shouted words of encouragement at him and continued getting high.

Once the song was over, Carmen told Allen that she was hot, so they both went outside for some fresh air.

"So did you have fun at your first 'in' party?" Carmen asked him, while taking a seat on the stoop outside the house.

Allen nodded his head and smiled, "Yeah, especially now that I'm getting the attention of Carmen Sanchez from the T.L.C.'s!"

"Ha, ha, ha, Allen. Real funny," she dryly retorted.

"But we both know it's true. You wouldn't be speaking to me unless I got to be this cool."

Carmen raised her eyebrows, "What are you talking about Allen? I speak to you every day."

"But not like this."

Carmen got quiet.

Allen broke the silence, "You never answered my question from earlier."

"What question?"

Allen's voice got smooth, "Are you feelin' me?"

Carmen moved in closer to Allen, "The question is, are you feeling me?"

"You already know, ma."

Both of them slowly moved their heads in closer and closer together until their lips touched. It was just a simple kiss, but to both of them, it felt like more. Carmen moved her head away from Allen's, "Sí."

"Sí?" Allen said, still in a daze from their kiss.

"Sí, I like you. Yes, I like you."

"Well, if you like me, how 'bout we hang out sometime soon."

Carmen looked at him funny, "Where exactly do you wanna 'hang out'?"

Allen shook his head and laughed, "Naw Carmen, not like that. I just wanna take you out."

"Where?"

"You'll see when the time comes," he learned that line from Marcus Hamilton.

"Fine," Carmen giggled.

Carmen stood up to go back into the house, and Allen followed suit. She went to go talk to her friends and he walked around a bit holding some short conversations, joking around with Torean and the Boys, and finally when he got bored, Allen snuck off and went to see if Mariah was still in the mood to make his night interesting.

It was silly for Allen to think that once he got Carmen, he was going to change back into the person that he once was.

Once a player, always a player is what his good friend Torean taught him. Allen liked the new him way too much to just transform back into the class clown so soon.

***

"Having fun?" Bryanna asked Torean once she walked up to the couch where the Clique Boys were getting high.

Torean smirked at Bryanna, eyes a dull red, "Yeah I was, but I don't mind having fun with you if that's what you want me to do."

"Well, you did invite me to this party, so I was expecting you to be a proper host," Bryanna didn't know why she actually came to this party. Actually, she did, but she was trying her hardest to find a different explanation other than the most apparent one. One thing that she did know for certain was that Torean looked unbelievably sexy with his Calvin Klein cable knit sweater and freshly cut hair.

Torean stood up from his seat and told his boys that he'd see them later. He placed his arm across Bryanna's bare shoulders and began to lead her into the kitchen where there was no one in there except some fat guy grabbing a fist full of potato chips.

"This brings back memories," Torean flirtatiously said, looking around the kitchen that reminded him of the time him and Bryanna had hooked up at Marcus's party a while back.

Bryanna rolled her eyes, "Horrible memories."

Torean snuggled her in closer to him, "Now, I know you didn't go through all this trouble to come to my function and then start talkin' that mess."

Bryanna laughed.

Torean took a short minute to devour her gorgeousness up with his eyes. Looking just like Rihanna with her shortened hair and golden skin, ignoring the cold weather, Bryanna wore a gray eighties inspired top, exposing her right shoulder. To cover her legs she wore leather leggings with black pumps on her pedicured feet.

"Now that's what I thought. So what do you wanna drink?" Torean said to his guest of honor.

She pointed to the side of the counter that held all the liquor you could possibly dream of, "Can I have a Mike's Hard Lemonade?"

Torean picked the alcohol up and handed it to her. She took it and gulped it down. Torean started to get excited. Hopefully she'll get tipsy again so that he can *really* have a good time.

"Aye, where yo' girl at?" asked Torean.

"Who Neisha?" Bryanna asked.

"Who else?" Torean smartly replied.

Bryanna ignored his comment, "Her and Trent wanted to go to the movies or whatever," though she tried to sound nonchalant, Torean could hear the slight twang of jealousy in her voice.

"So you came here all alone?"

"I was hoping to hang with you the entire night."

Torean raised his eyebrows, "Oh really?"

Torean quickly went back to the liquor and grabbed another lemonade for Bryanna.

"Drink up."

Bryanna took the bottle and smirked up at Torean, "What are you trying to do? Get me drunk so that you can take advantage of me?"

Torean chuckled and nestled his lips next to her ear, "What type of person do you think I am?"

Not letting the fact that Torean Hudson's famous lips were rubbing against her ear, Bryanna smartly replied, "The type of person who would get me drunk so that you could take advantage of me."

"Well since you clearly know me so well," Torean lightly said to Bryanna, moving his head away from hers, "how about we just skip the formalities and just get right down to business?"

Bryanna bit her lip and her shoulders rose up and down as she quietly laughed at Torean's bold request. She did come all the way to the party to hang out with him, so what would be so bad about giving in to temptation? He was beyond sexy, and by the looks of things, totally into her tonight. Bryanna chugged down the rest of her alcohol and smacked her lips together before saying, "Alright Torean, I'm in. But only on one condition."

Torean grinned, "What's that?"

"You have to keep this between you and me."

"Trust me," Torean said to Bryanna while taking her empty bottle and placing it on the counter, "my lips are sealed."

CARMEN SANCHEZ
Tuesday, 9:15p.m. ~ PARTY

"So what were you and pretty boy

doing outside?" Lauren asked Carmen after being outside with Allen.

Carmen gushed, "We kissed!"

"How was it?" Tiffany asked.

Carmen bit her lip, reminiscing, "It was simple and short, but it made me feel all warm and tingly inside," she put her hand over her heart in an over-dramatic manner.

Lauren and Carmen laughed.

Tiffany began to hate.

"Girl please," Tiffany said, "every boy with a pair of Jordans on makes you feel warm and tingly."

Carmen rolled her eyes towards the ceiling, but on their way up, they happened to fall on a tan guy with short hair who was leaving the main party area with a curly haired senior with thick hips. Carmen roughly flipped her hair over her shoulder and groaned with an attitude, "That boy has some nerve!"

Tiffany looked over at Allen disappearing and chuckled to herself. Carmen gave her a daggering stare, and she quickly got on the defense, "I mean it's not like you're his main girl anyway. You two only shared one kiss. And last I heard, you weren't even into Mr. Funny Man," Tiffany pouted her glossy lips like she just made three of the smartest points ever. Though Lauren didn't verbally say anything, she happened to agree with Tiffany. Single is single, and last she checked,

Allen was free to sneak off with whomever his whorish heart desired.

"Ugh guys! Can you be on my side for once?" Carmen replied, annoyed, "Allen just kissed me like twenty minutes ago, and just like that he forgot about me. *Me*, Carmen freaking Sanchez that fast, and walked away with some bald headed, too old for him, big booty girl! Does that even seem close to being fair?"

"Well," Lauren began to say, but Carmen quickly cut her off.

"I really thought that Allen of all people would be different. Torean truly has transformed him into his clone," she finger combed her hair in frustration, "Me siento como un idiota."

"Huh?" Tiffany and Lauren simultaneously said to Carmen.

Carmen crossed her arms and breathed out a depressing huff, "I feel like such an idiot."

"Look," Tiffany snapped at her friend, "can your foreign ass tell me where we are at right now?"

Confused, Carmen replied, "A party."

"Right! So why in the world is a fellow T.L.C. of mine crying over some player-for-a-day lame like Allen Rivera?"

"I'm not crying over anyone," Carmen replied in defense.

Tiffany put her brown hand up to silence her friend, "Look, just shut up. Look at you; look at *us*," Tiffany said, flicking her finger at her and her girls, "Every guy here wants us, and every girl here wants to be us. You are not allowed to stand here and pout over a guy. I don't care if it were Chris Brown who dissed you; you better go and show some of them pretty teeth to Trey Songz, girl."

That made Carmen laugh.

Tiffany continued, "Girls these days are so easy to cry over a guy. Get a clue, ain't none of them negros cryin' over any of our butts! So you need to stop trippin'," Tiffany put a cocky grin on her face, "I know guys who will most definitely get your mind off of Allen Rivera."

Going back into her T.L.C. mode, Carmen replied, "Like?"

Tiffany strutted off into the crowd and two minutes later came out with 6'2, bronzed skinned, narrow lipped guy who looked to be at least seventeen. He wore his hair in a fade, and unlike most of the guys at this party, he decided against wearing sneakers, but instead had on a mature pair of Sperry's on his feet.

Lauren whined, "Why does she always pick the really hot ones for you?"

Carmen put on her one-of-a-kind smile for the cutie and waited for him and Tiffany to approach her. Tiffany confidently walked up to her friends with the eye candy holding on to her hand.

"Carmen this is Mitchell. Mitchell, this is Carmen."

Mitchell looked directly into Carmen's eyes and smiled like a true gentleman. "I know exactly who she is. Nonetheless, it is such a pleasure to meet you Carmen," and he sealed his introduction by taking her hand and giving her a light kiss with his beautiful lips.

Carmen giggled warmly, "It's nice to meet you too."

Tiffany butted in, "Mitchell happens to be president of the junior class and the lead for the production of Othello."

Mitchell laughed.

"Oh, and did I forget to add that Mitchell is also a shoe-in for junior prom king?" Tiffany cooed as she grabbed Lauren by her dainty arm. The two of them rushed off into the crowd, giving Carmen and Mitchell some time alone.

"Sooo," Carmen said, quietly laughing at the awkward moment Tiffany left them with.

Mitchell didn't say anything; he was too busy staring at Carmen.

"Everything alright there?" she said to him, getting a little creeped out.

He gave a husky chuckle, "I'm sorry, but has anyone ever told you how beautiful you are?"

"Well besides my parents, you're the only one who has ever said that to me,"

Could this guy be any more of a gentleman? Carmen thought.

Mitchell grinned to himself and began to gaze off at the various things going on around the house party, "So how has your night been going so far?"

Thinking back to how she started her night off being grossed out by how girls were throwing themselves at Allen, then to how her night turned romantic when Allen admitted he liked her, and finally when her night turned horrible when she saw Allen running off with that skank; she was ready to say that her night absolutely sucked. But when Carmen looked up at Mitchell, all her bad emotions instantly went away, "Honestly," Carmen sweetly told Mitchell, "my night has most definitely taken a turn for the better."

ALLEN RIVERA
Monday, 11:30a.m. ~ CAFETERIA

"Where are you going?"

Patrick asked exasperatedly when he noticed Allen stand like he was about to go somewhere.

Allen was already walking when he told Patrick, "Imma go holler at the Clique Boys real quick, aight?"

"Sure man," Patrick replied, stuffing his sour cream and onion chips into his mouth with an attitude. This whole leaving the best friend behind thing was really starting to piss Patrick off.

Allen made his way to the lunch table where Torean, Marcus, Drew, and Ricky were all eating. Of course, there were females around too, but he wasn't complaining; he needed someone to hang out with after school before he went on his date tonight.

"Aye bro, what's good?" Torean said to Allen, giving him a fist bump when he came up to the table.

He was greeted with, "Hey Allen!" by all the females sitting around them.

Once Drew was done giving a play to Allen he said, "You hangin' out with us at Govern Park this afternoon?"

Govern Park? Allen thought. *That's the Clique Boy's hangout. No one gets to go there unless they're invited. I wonder what this means for my rep?*

Allen shook his head and replied, "Sorry bro, I can't make it."

Marcus raised his eyebrows, "What you got planned?"

Allen blew out some air and scratched his head, thinking, and finally answered, "Man I'm busy this entire week. I got Monica on Monday, Tina on Tuesday, Whitney on Wednesday, Tasha on Thursday, Falon on Friday, and Stacey on Saturday."

"What about Sunday?" Ricky curiously asked.

"I have to go to church," Allen replied seriously.

The Clique Boys all looked at each other and started cracking up laughing.

"What?" Allen asked, not getting the joke.

Torean stopped laughing long enough to say back to him, "Al, you might be a player now, but that does not stop you from still being hilarious! You're going to pass up on uhh, Sunday Sandra," Torean hypothetically said, "for *church*? You are one odd dude."

"Man, I have to go. My mom already thinks I'm acting weird. If I ever skip out on church she just might ship me off to Mexico to go live with my Abuela, and I am not trying to have that," Allen told his boys.

"I feel it," Drew replied, "You never wanna make the moms mad, but she's going to have to understand that you're popular now; what she thinks as weird, everyone sees as fly."

"True," said Torean.

Allen saw where his friends were coming from, but they didn't understand his parents the way he did. His mom and dad were used to Allen behaving one type of way for sixteen years straight, and for him to now all of a sudden switch up his personality on them had the two of them automatically assuming the worst. Even his best friend didn't understand him anymore. Allen knew it was going to take some time for everyone from his old life to get used to the new Allen, but he just wished they would hurry it up a bit because the brand new, popular ladies man was not going anywhere.

ALLEN RIVERA
Monday, 2:15p.m. ~ ANNOUNCEMENTS

Torean and Allen walked out of the
media productions classroom looking good. Both had on a simple pair of slacks and a button up with a tie. They made their way out of the classroom and into the green room to begin taping the announcements.

"Looking good Allen," a girl who helped tape the announcements said to him while walking past the two boys.

Allen smiled back at her and Torean shook his head.

"What?" Allen asked.

"These girls have been sweating the hell out of your jock!"

"I know man!" Allen said, laughing.

"What's so funny?" Carmen asked, walking up to them. She was dressed in a medium length yellow skirt and a white, ruffled, dressy blouse.

"Nothin', just tellin' Allen that these females are addicted to his ugliness."

Carmen laughed, "Ooo, Allen's not ugly. He's soooo adorable!" Carmen joked around, pinching Allen's cheek like she was an old lady.

Allen moved her hand out of the way and flirtatiously said, "I bet you really wanted to touch my face, didn't you?"

Torean laughed and went to sit at the wooden table.

"C'mon guys, it's time to start filming!" Kayla shouted to everyone in the room.

Carmen and Allen made their way over to the table, and when they sat down, Allen tried to continue the conversation, "I saw you talkin' to that lame Brad during Spanish today."

Carmen shrugged her shoulders, "And?"

"And that dude's weak as hell."

Kayla put her hands on her hips and shouted, clearly annoyed, "Can everyone shut up and get ready?"

Allen ignored her, "I thought you were feelin' me after what went down Friday night."

Carmen tissed, "I thought you were feeling me too, but I saw you going upstairs with Mariah, remember?"

Allen laughed, "We ain't do nothin' baby. She just...You know."

"No, I don't know," Carmen said, rolling her eyes.

"Neither do I," Torean chimed in.

"Shut up!" Kayla shouted again.

Allen put his hand up, signaling for Kayla to hush, and turned his head back to Carmen, "Look, you gon' do what you wanna do, and I'm gon' do what I wanna do. So let's just keep our side things to ourselves and when we do something together, *then* you can be askin' all those questions."

Carmen opened her mouth in disbelief and Torean turned his head away so that he could laugh.

"Are you serious Allen?"

"Serious as a heart attack."

Carmen gave a laugh like she couldn't believe what Allen had said, she stood up, and began to walk away from the table.

"Are you serious right now?" Kayla said exasperatedly as she watched Carmen walk away from the set.

Allen stood up and ran towards Carmen. "Carmen, wait up!" he said, grabbing her arm, halting her from walking away.

"What?"

"Why are you mad at me?"

She folded her arms and replied sourly, "Because, you're treating me like these other guys treat me and I thought you were different."

"I am different."

"No. You're just like every other player at this school."

"Let me prove it to you," Allen said smiling, trying to convince her that he was a good guy.

"How are you going to prove it to me?" Carmen asked unconvinced.

"I wanna take you out."

Carmen nonchalantly asked, "When?"

Allen pulled out his cell phone, looking at his schedule, "I'm free next Saturday."

Carmen rolled her eyes, "*Next* Saturday?"

Allen flirtatiously grinned and backed her into the corner of the room where no one could see them, "I'm gonna do whatever it takes to show you that I'm better than any of those dudes that you've been talking to."

"Is that right?"

Allen licked his lips, "Yeah."

Carmen laughed half-heartedly, "So you really think that you can be better than the dude I'm talking to?"

"Yes the—" Allen paused once Carmen's statement fully registered in his brain, "Wait," he said, "*Dude?* What you mean?"

Carmen moved from under Allen and allowed a mean grin to spread across her pretty face, "I mean I'm with someone Allen."

"Ah hahahahaha!" Allen laughed and bent over with his hand against a wall to support him, "I didn't know you had some jokes on you!"

Carmen put some lips gloss on her lips, "I'm being serious Allen. I'm dating Mitchell Tucker now."

"That actor kid?"

"Yes, him," Carmen replied, pouting her lips into her compact mirror.

Allen shook his head in disbelief, "When did you have time to date him when you were just kissing me two days ago?"

Carmen scowled at him, "Funny the things someone can do after sharing a kiss," at that, she sauntered away from Allen. Almost in a daze from the shocking news he just received, Allen followed Carmen back into the media room. The two were greeted by the eyes of a curious Torean Hudson.

Torean looked expectantly at Allen, waiting for some sort of sign to show him that he had Carmen in the bag, but all he got was a confused and ego-hurt look from Allen, while a cocky grin was plastered on Carmen's face for the entire school to see.

The three of them looked into the camera, some more cheerful than others, and prepared to tape the announcements for Tuesday morning.

"Finally!" Kayla mumbled under her breath.

Allen could not wait to be done with the announcements for today. The longer he had to be around Carmen, the more depressed he was sure to become. What was even worse was the fact that he couldn't even express the way he felt because that would make him look like a chump in front of his friend and his almost-girl.

ALLEN RIVERA
Monday, 4:23p.m. ~ BEDROOM

Allen spun around in his computer chair
and stared out into the Wisconsin cold from his window.

"Today is officially going down as one of the worst days of my high school life," he said to himself. Finding out that the girl who he did all this work for ended up falling for someone else really sucked. He really thought that they were making progress when they kissed the night of the party. He understood that he probably should have made his sneak off with Mariah a little more low key; maybe then none of this would have happened.

Allen knew that Mitchell Tucker was not the guy for Carmen. *Allen* was. Mitchell was always trying to act so romantic and mature. Allen knew it's all a front. No seventeen-year-old guy in his right mind would seriously walk around a high school wearing bowties and Dockers on the daily, belt out Shakespeare just for the heck of it, and buy flowers for a girl he just started dating.

"Ugh!" the thought of what happened earlier that day made Allen sick. He couldn't help but relive that moment over:

At 3:29p.m. in the parking lot of Wilson High School, Allen sat in his Chevy, blasting his Watch the Throne album. He hoped that some good hip hop would get his mind off of the fact that Carmen now had a boyfriend.

"Shoot," Allen mumbled after he dropped his cell phone from out of his hand. He reached down to pick it up, and as he was on the return, he knocked his head against the steering wheel, causing his horn to go off. A few teenagers who were still outside, looked at Allen. Three of them happened to be Tiffany Rodgers, Lauren Daniels, and Carmen Sanchez.

Allen couldn't help but watch the group of girls. The T.L.Cs walked over to Lauren's Hybrid and placed their matching North Face backpacks into the trunk of the car. After Lauren closed her trunk, she looked over to the left and started to "awww" at something. Allen turned his head to see what she was looking at.

He gripped his steering wheel so tight that his knuckles turned white.

Mitchell strode up to the group of girls with a single red rose in his bronze hand. Carmen wore the biggest grin on her face and once he finally approached her, she wrapped her arms around him and gave him a nice smooch on his lips. Pulling back from Carmen, Mitchell handed Carmen the rose, and said something that Allen couldn't quite make out. Whatever he said made the girls gush though.

But then the worst part came.

Once Mitchell handed the red rose to Carmen, he broke out in melody, singing an acapella version of "Superstar" by Usher. Allen heard him sing the song with such talent and it pissed him off more and more with every line of the song the guy sang. Allen saw Tiffany and Lauren lightly jump up and down in excitement, so once again Allen looked over to the left. Coming towards Carmen were five guys. Each one of them was singing the same song and carried a bouquet of red roses. Carmen fanned herself from being so overwhelmed with sweetness.

I'll be your groupie baby, 'cause you are my superstar. And as your number one fan, I'll do all that I can, to show you how super you are.

The six well-dressed guys harmonized the last line of the song, and Mitchell finished it off by kissing Carmen on her hand.

Tiffany and Lauren eagerly took the roses from the handsome boys and placed them into the car, "You coming with?" Tiffany asked Carmen. She seemed to be mesmerized by Mitchell Tucker. Still staring him in his hazel eyes, she replied, "I think I'm just going to have Mitchell take me home today."

Lauren and Tiffany naughtily glanced at each other before saying to their friend, "Okay girl," and hopped into the Hybrid.

Allen took that as his queue to leave, so he restarted the engine to his car. The noise of the start-up caught the attention of Carmen. Allen looked at her with bothered eyes, and Carmen gave him a bitchy smile behind Mitchell's back in return. She grabbed onto her boyfriend even tighter, and allowed him to lead her off to his car, the rose that he gave her still held in her hand.

Everything I did was all for nothing, Allen thought, still staring out his window and spinning in his computer chair. All the lessons he learned, all the rules he had to memorize, all the money he spent on clothes; was it really all for nothing? As soon as he had hope that the girl of his dreams was actually interested in him, she turned around and spat in his face. Maybe he was better off just being a dorky funny-guy after all.

Allen's new iPhone began to vibrate. He looked at the caller ID and saw that it was an unknown number. Wanting to focus his attention on anything other than Carmen Sanchez, he answered his phone.

"Hello?"

Guuuh guuuh ahhh guh.

"Hello?" Allen said once again.

"Hay der baybay!"

"Oh my God…please don't tell me this is—"

"Boo, it's Lafonda!" she grunted into the phone.

Allen wiped his face with his free hand, in disbelief that Lafonda Rice was actually on the phone with him.

"Ain't you happy tew heya mah voice?"

"What do you want Lafonda?"

She loudly laughed into the phone and Allen had to pull it away from his ear so that she wouldn't injure his eardrum.

"I'm hongrey. Yer got any fewd at yer howse?"

"Why in the hell do you think I would feed you?"

Lafonda got quiet for a second, "Becuz yew my boo thang."

Allen couldn't help but laugh at Lafonda. This girl meant no harm to him. All she wanted was some attention. And he had to admit that she was keeping his mind off of Carmen.

"Okay Lafonda," Allen said, "Hypothetically speaking, if I was to cook you a meal, what would you want me to make for you?"

"Oh boy! I don't know if yew can handle dis!" Lafonda excitedly said to Allen. He heard her breathing accelerate at the thought of food.

Allen chuckled a bit more, "I have nothing but time."

ALLEN RIVERA & TOREAN HUDSON
Wednesday 1:19p.m. ~ SOPHOMORE HALLWAY

Leaning on the lockers, the Clique

Boys, along with Allen, were chilling around before they went to their next class.

"You ever get that research paper done for Biology?" Drew asked Torean.

"Yeah, I got Kayla to help me with it," Torean replied.

"Dang, I shoulda thought of that," Drew groaned.

"And you should've thought about wearing something else to school today!" Ricky joked to his friend. Drew, Torean, and Allen laughed at Ricky's diss. Drew was fascinated with eighties fashion. Coming to school in white skinny jeans, a black v-neck under a fire truck red Member's Only jacket, oversized nerd glasses, and a pair of Jordan I's on his feet, Drew thought, along with 99.9% of the girls at school, that he looked fresh to death. Drew did not take Ricky's words to heart. Not one bit.

"Aww Mitchell you are so sweet!" Allen heard down the hallway.

He tried not to listen to what was going on, but once the couple made their way past the friends; he had no choice but to see the two in action. Allen watched as Mitchell and Carmen walked hand in hand down the hallway. All eyes were on the glamorous couple, including Allen's. They stopped at

Carmen's locker and he grabbed her books from it. She stood there smiling at his polite gesture. After picking up her things for her next class, Carmen pulled the collar of his Ralph Lauren polo until his face reached her lips. The couple shared a lustful kiss before walking back off, hand in hand, to Carmen's next class.

Allen watched the two walk until they were out of eyesight. Carmen and Mitchell had dated for a week now, and every day that has passed, Allen wanted to punch Mitchell more and more. He and Carmen hadn't spoke a word to each other since the day where she told Allen about her new boyfriend. Speaking or not speaking, Allen wanted Carmen to be his. Seeing her with someone else didn't just make him jealous, it made him unbelievably miserable.

"What's up Tor?" Bryanna walked up to Torean. Neisha close behind.

"Hey baby," Torean smoothly said to Bryanna. He moved his eyes onto Neisha, "Hey ugly."

"Haha," Neisha dryly retorted.

"What's good with you?" he asked the beautiful Bryanna Wilson.

"Nothing, just on my way to class."

"You gon' let me walk you there?" Torean asked, smiling softly while he ran his finger on her cheek.

Bryanna laughed, "The last thing I want is for people to see you walking me down the hall. Who knows the rumors they might start?"

"I can think of a few," Torean said mischievously.

Neisha rolled her eyes, "Pulease!"

"Shut up Neisha!" Ricky, Drew, Torean, and Allen all said.

"Anyway," Torean said to Bryanna, "You down for me taking you to class or what?"

Bryanna squished her face like she was in deep thought, "I guess it wouldn't hurt too much for you to walk me. Just don't touch me or anything."

"Now you know I can't be around you for more than two minutes without my hands feeling on your body," Torean flirted with Bryanna.

She couldn't help but giggle, "Shut up and just take me to class."

"You know I like it when you talk rude to me," Torean snatched up Bryanna's books and walked with her down the hallway while Neisha slowly followed behind, her face showing a distinct sign of annoyance because she looked like the third wheel while her best friend was cuffed up with a Clique Boy.

CARMEN SANCHEZ
Wednesday, 9:26 am ~ SOPHOMORE HALLWAY

Carmen wiped the smile off her face

as soon as she rounded the empty corner of the hallway, "Look," she said to Mitchell, "I can't do this anymore."

"What do you mean?"

"I mean that this whole making Allen jealous by dating you scam isn't working out anymore," Carmen finger combed her hair in thought, "I think he caught the hint. Plus, this," she moved her finger at the both of them, "definitely isn't fun anymore."

The night that Carmen met Mitchell, she came up with the idea of paying him twenty dollars a day to pretend to be her boyfriend. Mitchell took on the challenge, seeing it as a way to sharpen his acting skills, and he handled the job like a professional. Even though he had been feeling Carmen, he was feeling that money she was offering him a whole lot more. The plan was to keep up the act for a month, so when Carmen said she wanted to throw in the towel after only one week, he couldn't help but to become suspicious.

Mitchell scratched his head while he chuckled to himself, "Do you really think he caught the hint, or is it just that you don't want him to move on too fast?"

Carmen smiled at Mitchell, "Maybe a little bit of both. But don't you dare tell anyone."

Mitchell put both his hands up in defense, "Hey, your secret is safe with me."

"Perfect."

Mitchell handed Carmen's books to her, relieved to no longer have to carry her heavy textbooks around anymore. Grabbing her dainty hand, he said smoothly, "It was a pleasure doing business with you," and sweetly kissed her on her hand. He turned from her and began walking away. Once he was a few feet down the hall, Mitchell abruptly stopped and paced back to Carmen.

Oh boy, Carmen thought, *he better not be coming back over here to tell me he actually caught real feelings for me*. That was most definitely the last thing she wanted. Mitchell Tucker was cool and all, but by no means was he her type.

Coming up very close to her, Carmen looked up apprehensively at her pretend ex boyfriend.

"Yo, can I get my last twenty you owe me?" Mitchell asked, his hand held out expectantly.

Carmen rolled her eyes, "Here," she said, pulling a twenty out of her back pocket.

He smiled as he quickly snatched the money out of her hand and skipped down the hallway. Carmen switched the weight of her books to her other arm as she continued on her way to class, happy to be done with getting back at Allen for being such a player.

ALLEN RIVERA
Friday, 10:20a.m. ~ SPANISH II

Torean was already comfortable in
his seat when he saw Allen walk in looking disgruntled.

"Aye, what's wrong man?" Torean asked his friend.

Allen slammed himself into the seat next to Torean, "Man, I cannot handle this anymore! Everything we did was to get

Carmen to pay attention to me, but now she is ignoring more than she did when I was the class clown. Her attitude is really starting to irritate me!"

"Hold the hell up," Torean said to Allen, placing his hand on his shoulder, "Are you really telling me that you're getting heated over a *girl*?"

Allen guiltily mumbled.

"What is rule number twenty Al?" Torean asked.

Allen answered quietly, "Rule number twenty: players never stop being a player."

"So tell me why in the world are you losing your cool over a girl? When you saw that Carmen was with someone else, you should've made sure that Carmen never saw you sweat. Boy, you should've made sure that she knew that you didn't need her."

Allen snapped, "I don't *need* her. I just want her."

Torean mischievously grinned, "And if a player wants something?"

"I get it. Plain and simple," Allen replied confidently.

Torean cocked his head in the direction of the door, "Look who just came through."

Allen got up from his seat and ran his hand over his freshly cut head. He walked up to the unbelievably gorgeous Carmen Sanchez, wearing an oversized sweater, leggings and Uggs, and grabbed her arm, leading her out of the classroom.

"Allen! What the heck are you doing?" Carmen shouted in surprise.

"Look here," Allen cockily said, "you are gonna dump that lame that you're with and tomorrow you will be going out on a date with me. We clear?"

Carmen gave him a half smirk, "Crystal clear," she moved her arm out of Allen's grip and walked back into the classroom.

CHARMANE WHITE

Allen couldn't help but show all his teeth when he walked into the Spanish II classroom a little after Carmen came in.

"Yo, how did it go?" Torean curiously asked.

"I told her the deal and she agreed without any fight," Allen leaned back in his chair and put his hands behind his head in confident relaxation.

Torean patted Allen on the back, "That's my boy! You showed her whose boss!"

Carmen snickered to herself, listening to everything the two boys were saying.

If they only knew.

ALLEN RIVERA
Friday, 8:16p.m. ~ BEDROOM

"What up ma?"

She giggled from the other end of the phone, "Hey Allen, what's up?"

"Nothin' really, just tryna see what you on for later tonight," Allen suavely replied.

"Hmmm," the she breathed, "I have nothing planned…unless you're trying to change that for me?"

Allen huskily laughed, "I'm always down for making someone's night better."

"Is that right?"

"Fa sho. I mean real talk, you were looking fine as hell in Spanish today. If you still looking that good right now, I'm definitely down to have you come through."

Allen listened to her giggle.

"Hold on a second," Allen waited a few minutes until she got back on the phone.

"Hello?" she said.

"I'm here sexy."

"Did you get my picture?"

Allen looked at his phone, and saw that he had a new picture mail. He opened the message and looked at her posing on her bed, wearing a black push up bra with a zebra stripped thong. Her long hair looked so sexy and her thick lips were turning him on just from the thought of what she could do with them.

"I got the pic," Allen finally replied.

"Well?" she said expectantly.

"Was that picture just taken or is that something you had stored in your phone?" Allen boldly asked.

"Why does it matter?"

"Because," Allen replied, "I only accept originals. And if you're sending me a copied picture, then that makes me wonder how many guys have seen this one."

"It was an original Allen. No need to worry."

"Girl please, worrying is something I do not do."

The other line was quiet for a while.

"Hello?" she said after a while

Allen rolled his eyes in annoyance, "You comin' over or what?"

"Let me throw some clothes on and I'll be there in a second," the girl excitedly answered.

"Nah, what you had on in that picture was good. No need to put on unnecessary clothes when I'm gonna end up taking them off of you as soon as you walk through the door," Allen surprised himself with how much he sounded like Torean Hudson.

The girl laughed, "Okay, I'll be over there in a bit."

"Sounds like a plan," he replied, getting horny at the thought of seeing her amazing body in person.

"Bye Allen."

"Peace Rachael."

Allen hung up from Rachael and scrolled through his many contacts until he reached the C's. Selecting Carmen's name, he sent her a text message.

Just wanted to let you know how much im lookin forward 2 our date tomorrow. If u up, shoot me a text ;)

Allen locked his phone and got himself ready for the company he was about to have tonight.

CARMEN SANCHEZ & ALLEN RIVERA
Saturday, 6:00pm
WESTOWNE MOVIE THEATER

Allen stood by the entrance of the movie theater watching Carmen walk across the parking lot. Allen's eyes popped out of his head when he saw her. She was wearing white ripped, skinny jeans, a grey cami with a light pink long sleeved v-neck shirt, and on her feet were a pair of grey moccasins. Her hair was wavy, and her makeup was PERFECT. Carmen looked good, and Allen wasn't afraid to let her know it.

"Wow girl, you look amazing," Allen slowly said, looking her up and down.

Carmen showed her pearly whites and told him, "Right back at ya, sexy."

Allen had on some faded, form-fitting A&F jeans, a white t-shirt under a mild yellow and white striped polo, with plain white Jordans. With his collar up and a fresh haircut, Carmen just couldn't keep her eyes off him.

"C'mon, let's go inside," Allen said, opening the door to the theater.

With Allen's long arm around Carmen's shoulder, they stopped at the ticket booth, where they were greeted by a cheerful attendant.

"Hi, welcome to Westowne Movie Theater. What movie would you like to see today?" the happy guy said behind the booth.

"What do you wanna see?" Allen asked.

Carmen bit her lip in thought as the man behind the booth began checking her out. "Can we get two tickets for 'One Bad Night'?"

"Sure thing," he perkily replied.

Allen raised his eyebrows, "You sure you're not gonna get scared?"

Carmen wrapped her arm around Allen's waist and replied, "If I get scared, I'll just ask you to comfort me."

Allen smiled and gave her a Torean-Worthy wink, "You already know I don't have a problem with doing that."

And with that, the two of them made their way into the screening room.

***

"That movie sucked!" Allen told Carmen, "It was a typical slasher movie. No originality."

"Oh, shut up Allen, I liked it. That's all that matters."

Allen walked Carmen over to his car. Tiffany had dropped her off earlier, so he took her home. But it was only eight o'clock...

"It was a waste of money if you ask me."

Carmen rolled her eyes and said sarcastically, "Oh yeah Allen, you spent a whole twenty dollars on movie tickets, and we didn't even have popcorn. You were spending big tonight!"

Allen laughed while opening the car door for her. As she got in, he rubbed his hand across her butt. At the touch, Carmen turned around to look at Allen, but he was already making his way to the driver's side of the car. Once they were inside, he turned his radio up, letting Beyonce's "Ego" play softly through the speakers.

While Carmen sang along to the song, Allen looked over at her and said, "Do you have a big ego?"

She smiled at him "I guess so. I *am* a T.L.C."

"So you think that just because you're a T.L.C., you have to have a big ego?"

"No, I'm saying that because I'm a T.L.C., I have a big ego."

Allen smiled, "Okay, I bet you just think that you're the bomb, right?"

"Well you wanted to get at me, didn't you?"

Allen laughed.

"Now it's my turn to ask if you have a big ego or not."

"It depends on which ego you're talking about," Allen joked.

Carmen mischievously giggled, "Both."

Allen lowered the volume down while turning down the street to Carmen's neighborhood.

"Well, my ego-ego really isn't that big, seeing as how I just started becoming this way a few weeks ago. But my *ego* is pretty damn big if I say so myself."

Carmen rolled her eyes, "Yeah, you're not the only person who thinks you have a big ego."

Allen turned to her questioningly.

"You should know who I'm talking about, seeing as how you let her give you a blow job."

Allen smiled flirtatiously at Carmen. He thought it was too sexy seeing her hate on the females that talked to him.

"You can suck my dick too, if you wanna see what the ladies are talking about."

"Allen, if I wanted you, I could've had you by now."

He pulled near the curb of Carmen's small house. Once he put the car in park, he turned to her and said, "Apparently you wanted me; that's why we're together now."

"Oh yeah?" Carmen said sarcastically.

Allen smoothly leaned into Carmen, ran his fingers across her cheek, and said, "Yeah," before kissing her slow and passionately on the lips. Carmen pulled away so that she could get some air, and Allen placed his hand on her neck, pulling her back in for another kiss. The longer they kissed, the rougher they became with each other. Their make-out was getting so hot and heavy that the windows were getting foggy.

Allen's big hands began to roam Carmen's body. He went from her face, to her chest, down to her stomach, where he went up her shirt. Carmen's breathing started to quicken, but Allen could tell that she didn't want to stop. He moved his hands on her thighs, where he rubbed them aggressively. He pulled Carmen over to his lap in the driver's seat, and began to kiss her on her neck. This turned Allen on very much. At that moment, he was happy that he practiced on so many girls because now he knew exactly what he wanted to do with Carmen.

Carmen started to nibble on his ear and say some pretty dirty things to him in Spanish. Allen moved his hands across her skinny jeans as he began to unzip them. He started to feel on her panties while she continued to egg him on in Spanish. Allen's hands found the spot that both of them wanted him to touch. Carmen moaned into his neck while Allen continued to finger her. It felt so good, she didn't want it to end.

When they were done, Carmen zipped back up her pants, and Allen tried to wipe off the satisfied look on his face.

Carmen kissed him good-bye, and climbed out of the car, sexily walking up the steps to her house. Once she opened the door, she gave Allen a wave good-bye, and he drove off.

A couple of minutes later, his cell phone went off. He pulled it out and it showed a text message from Carmen.

CarmenS.

9:00PM

I owe u 1...

Allen could barely hold in his excitement as he drove home. He was very curious to see what Carmen had up her sleeve for the next time they hung out. So curious in fact, that he was contemplating canceling his date Sunday evening with a girl who was sure to blow his mind multiple times in one night, just so he could get some alone time with Carmen Sanchez again.

THE CLIQUE BOYS
Saturday, 6:00p.m. ~ MARCUS'S GARAGE

"Turn the beat up louder!"

Torean shouted to Marcus. They were all in Marcus's garage trying to find the perfect beat for a new song

The Clique Boys were not only a bunch of players, but they were also a rap group. They went by the name of S.W.A.G., and the title suited them well. The four guys had flow as good as J. Cole and rapped out sexy verses that always got the ladies hot and bothered. The Clique Boy's parents said that they were too young to go out for a record deal, so they mostly just made demos until they turned eighteen and could then go for the record deal at Jive.

After they were done laying down their verses, they all sat around on the miss-matched chairs all over the garage. Ricky was sitting in a metal, fold-out chair. Sliding his phone back down, he said, "Allen is a trip!"

Marcus turned his head, "What went down?"

"Allen just told me that Tuesday Tina had sucked his dick in his car after school!"

All the guys started laughing and Torean said, "Man, I gotta get with her!"

"Oh yeah!" they shouted back in agreement.

"Dude, Allen has been snatchin' up plenty of girls," Drew said to his friends, still shaking his head at the news Ricky told them.

"That's my man!" Torean shouted, happy that his boy was becoming such a mack.

Drew rolled his eyes upward and said, "And your *man* is grabbin' all the girls at our school. Torean, you created a monster!"

"Whatever," Torean replied, swatting his hand at Drew.

Marcus added himself in, "It's true though. Those females are going crazy over that guy. I heard Cassie tell her friend that Allen is the finest guy at our school and that when she goes out with him, she's gonna give him some."

All the guys raised their eyebrows in disbelief. Torean was the first, as always, to speak, "You mean senior Cassie? The chick who wouldn't even let *me* hit when I took her out?"

"Yeah, that Cassie."

Torean shook his head, "Dang, I didn't know he was getting his game on so hard."

"I know, right!" Ricky said, "Allen doesn't even do his comedy roasts anymore. All he does is shop, hang out with us, and hook-up with the sexiest girls at Wilson."

"But it's only been a few weeks though."

"A few weeks is all it takes man. Once word gets around that you're the newest edition to the Wilson High Players, all the females wanna have a go at you," Drew said.

Marcus leaned down in his chair so that he was closer to the group, "Alright, now Allen has been going out on dates with girls every day of the week. When's the last time anyone of us has done something like that?"

"But you're dating Lynda," Ricky interjected.

Marcus put his hand up to hush Ricky.

"I don't know about you," Torean said, "but I still get pussy."

"But do you get it like Allen?" Drew asked smiling.

Torean cocked his head to the side, "What are you tryna say?"

"I'm sayin' that Allen's tryna steal your crown."

Torean tissed, "No one is gonna steal my crown. Watch this," Torean pulled out his cell phone from his Nike hoodie and scrolled through his contacts.

What the heck is everyone thinking? Just because Allen has some new clothes, talks different, and knows how to bag girls, that doesn't mean he's better than me. I mean, I'm the leader of the Clique Boys.

After the third ring, the phone picked up. Torean put his phone on speaker.

"Hello?" came the voice of a girl.

"What's goin' on Sherrie?" Torean said flirtatiously into the phone.

"Who is this?"

Torean cleared his throat uncomfortably, "It's me. Torean."

"Oh, hey Torean. I haven't heard from you in a while. What do you want?" Sherrie asked curiously.

Torean motioned for his boys to listen up, "I wanna hang out with you for a little bit tonight."

The other line was quiet for a while.

"Hello?" Torean spoke into the phone.

"Umm, I'm sorry Tor, but I already have plans to go out with Allen Rivera tonight," Sherrie replied apologetically.

"It's cool," Torean sucked his teeth while hanging up the phone.

The Clique Boys all tried to act like what they just heard with Sherrie was not a big deal, but it was hard to play that one off. It was apparent to everyone that Allen was becoming more popular than the Clique Boys thought. And most importantly, Torean's crown might actually be in danger.

CHARMANE WHITE

TOREAN HUDSON
Saturday, 11:03pm ~ TOREAN'S BEDROOM

Laying in darkness and silence,
Torean was bored out of his mind. This had to be the first Saturday ever in his life that he wasn't at a party. He just wasn't in the mood to deal with certain people at this point. And by certain people, he meant Allen Rivera. How could his player rep be in jeopardy after only a few weeks? It seemed like as soon as Allen Rivera came on the scene, the ladies had been lining up to have a go at him. Of course, Torean could still get girls, but it was harder now because the same chicks that wanted him were the same girls that wanted Allen. Basically, it was like he and Allen had to race to see who can get at the girl before the other person did. This whole predicament frustrated Torean because none of this seemed fair. Torean only wanted to turn Allen into a player so that he could have Carmen. But it was like now that he had Carmen, he still didn't want to stop doing what he was doing. Torean was not trying to player hate on him or anything, but he was just worried that his status might be in danger.

Torean flopped over on his stomach and blew out air. No way was he going to just lay around thinking about Allen Rivera all day. He needed someone to talk to…

Ring. Ring. Ring.

"Hello?" Bryanna asked. She was in her room, listening to Pleasure P's "Boyfriend #2", and lying on her bed. When she saw Torean's name pop up on her cell phone, at first she was excited because she hadn't talked to him since Friday morning, but remembering that she didn't act thirsty over any guy, she let the phone ring three times before answering it.

"Hey Bre. What you up to?" Torean heard music playing and thought she was at the party, but he wanted to make sure first.

Bryanna turned on her back and pressed the power button on her radio remote to cut the music off, "Nothing really, just chilling in my room."

"Oh, me too."

"Why didn't you go to Brian Miller's party tonight?"

Torean tried to look for a good excuse, "'Cause Brian's too lame to know how to throw a bangin' party."

Bryanna laughed, "You are such a hater!"

"I'm just speakin' the truth," Torean then asked her, "So why didn't you go?"

"I didn't go because Neisha and Trent went together, and I didn't feel like being the third wheel."

Torean got quiet. He could tell that the whole "Neisha and Trent" thing made Bryanna sad because she didn't have a man, but he didn't know what he was supposed to say.

"It's cool though," Bryanna tried to convince Torean, "I've been to too many parties this week anyway."

"I know that's right!" Torean agreed.

"So what did you *really* call for?" Bre asked.

Torean laughed into the phone, "I just wanted to talk ma. That's all."

"Mmhmm."

"For real girl. I haven't talked to you in a minute, and I just wanted to see what was up."

Bryanna rolled her eyes and said, "Tor, I know you well enough to know that you never call a girl just to see what was up."

"But you're not just any girl."

"Yeah Torean. Real funny."

"Do I look like Allen to you? I'm not jokin' around. I just wanted someone to talk to."

Bryanna tissed unbelievingly, "Okay then, what do you wanna talk about?"

The other end of the line got quiet while Torean thought of something to say. "I wanna talk about how horny I am."

"What?"

"You heard what I said."

"Whatever Torean. You're lucky I'm bored."

"So, are you going to let me say what's on my mind?"

"Yeah," Bryanna *trying* to sound annoyed because she was as much into talking dirty as Torean was. She just didn't want to let him know that.

Torean put on his award-winning flirtatious voice and said, "Can I have phone sex with you?"

There was a long pause on the phone until Bryanna finally answered, "Yes."

He got into his player mode and started off the convo, "What are you wearing?"

Bryanna tried to get into her sexy mode, "I have on a lavender underwear set under my white nightdress."

"Is it see-through?" Torean asked huskily.

"Yeah. I wish you were here to see it," She replied naughtily.

Torean started to get aroused, "Me too baby."

Bryanna asked, "What would you do to me if you were here?"

"Mmm," Torean moaned, "You really wanna know?"

Bryanna bit her lip and said, sounding turned on, "Tell me."

"I wanna lick you in all the right places, have you moan my name, begging me to go further. Then I want to ease deep inside of you and rock your world."

"You wanna do all those dirty things to me?" Bryanna sexily asked.

"Yeah," Torean breathed into the phone.

"Well too bad you're not going to!" Bryanna told Torean, putting her regular voice back on.

Torean got mad at her for playing around like that, "C'mon now girl! How you gone do me like that? I told you I was horny, then you gon' play with my emotions."

"Oh, shut up Torean. Did you really think I wanted to have phone sex with you?" Bryanna asked.

Torean rolled his eyes. He was tired of this hot-n-cold crap she did with him.

"Whatever girl. I know you liked it. That's why you waited until I told you some freaky stuff before you pulled the plug on me."

"Okay Torean, whatever you say."

"But for real though girl, I want you tonight," Torean flirtatiously said to Bryanna.

"Boy it's late, and my parents are home," she explained.

"It's only 10:45 on a Saturday night," he corrected.

"But my parents are still home."

Torean raised his eyebrows and asked, "So if your parents weren't home, could I have come over?"

Bryanna thought for a while and simply said, "Maybe. Maybe not."

"Why don't you come over my house?"

"Are your parents home?"

"My sister is over her friend's house, and my grandma has been asleep since six."

Bryanna rolled her eyes, "I'm not coming over your house just because your grandma's sleep."

"My gran can sleep through any noise."

"What kinda noise do you think we'll be making?" she asked.

Torean seductively said, "I think we both know the answer to that."

Bryanna laughed because she knew it was true.

"How about this," Bryanna suggested, "Why don't we both get dressed to impress and go to Brian's party together. That way if we get in the mood, we can go into one of his bedrooms."

Torean thought about her idea for a quick minute and then said, "Cool. I'll pick you up at eleven-thirty."

Bryanna smiled, "Okay."

"And Bryanna," Torean said.

"Yeah?"

"You better make this party worth my while."

"Bye Torean," Bryanna said, laughing and shaking her head as she hung up the phone.

It was always better to show up late than never. No one wanted to stay home on a Saturday night. And definitely not Torean.

Thursday, 8:00am

ANNOUNCEMENTS

"Don't forget about the Fall Ball this Friday at seven. No ticket purchase necessary. Just bring a date and your best dance moves!" Carmen said, winking into the camera lens.

THE CLIQUE BOYS

Thursday, 8:50am ~ SOMPHMORE HALLWAY

"Im thinking about asking Tee-Tee to the dance Friday," Ricky said to his friends. The Clique Boys were all standing around their lockers, as usual, before the warning bell rang.

"Why Tee-Tee?" Marcus asked. Tee-Tee was a freshman who was known around the school as the girl all the upperclassmen hit and quit.

Ricky replied, "Because I'm tryna get some easy sex."

Marcus laughed and the two of them joined in a play.

Torean tapped Drew on the shoulder and asked, "Who you goin' with?"

Drew got all smug and replied, "Lauren from the T.L.C.'s asked me to go with her."

"What?" All the guys asked in unison.

"Yeah, she texted me right after the announcements and asked me to roll with her."

"Dang man," Torean said, "You already know Lauren's gonna drop them panties."

Drew nodded his head, grinning from ear to ear. Then he turned his head towards Marcus and said, "Let me guess, you're goin' with Lynda, right?"

"You already know," Marcus replied. But he didn't really seem too happy about it.

"What you sound like that for? You acting like you gotta go with Lafonda Rice or something," Ricky smartly said to Marcus.

The Clique Boys started cracking up laughing.

"Yo, ol' girl bad as hell, I don't know what y'all talkin' 'bout," Marcus sarcastically replied.

Drew laughed, "Was it the dirt stains that got you turned on?"

"Or the gelled ponytail?"

"Naw, the sexy way she eat those Big Texas and how the top of her body is big but the bottom half is small. And don't get me started on her teeth!" Marcus said to his boys, pretending to be infatuated with Lafonda.

Torean laughed at his friend's jokes, "Y'all going to hell for that."

"Haha," Ricky laughed, "But who you going to the Fall Ball with?"

"I was sure that everyone knew by now that I'm goin' with Bryanna," Torean said to his boys. All of them raised their eyebrows, clearly they had not got the memo that him and Bryanna Wilson were going to the Fall Ball together.

"Since when did her stuck-up butt decide to go anywhere with *you*?" Ricky asked.

"Since she got a taste of Mr. Torean Hudson," he replied mischievously.

Marcus got excited, "She let you hit that?"

Torean swatted his hand at him and said, "Do I look like the type of guy who kisses and tells?"

All his friends looked at one another, then back at Torean and said, "Hell—"

What sounded like a stampede of hounds, reached the sophomore hallway.

Everyone, including Torean had turned their heads to see what the commotion was. There were at least ten of the finest girls in the middle of the hallway, and in the middle of the group stood Allen Rivera. The Clique Boys stood quietly, trying to ear hustle on everything that was being said.

"Ladies, ladies, ladies, calm down!" Allen said to the group of females that were surrounding him, "Now can you guys tell me what you want?"

One of the girls from the group, Victoria, came closer to him and said, "I was wondering if you wanted to go to the dance with me?"

"But I was going to ask you if you wanted to go to the dance with me first!" Mariah shouted at the two.

Another girl emerged from the circle and said, "Why would he want to go to the dance with you broke tricks, when he can go with me?" Shaniquia said, walking closer to Allen.

"He doesn't want to go to the dance with you; he wants to go with me!" Victoria shouted at the girls.

"Well, me and him had such a good time at that party, so I'm sure he'd rather go with *me*."

Allen put his hands up in protest, even though he loved every minute of this. He was truly starting to understand what it felt like to be Justin Bieber.

"I know a way that we can resolve this."

The girls all crossed their arms and asked, "How?"

Allen leaned against his locker and smoothly said, "Whoever can kiss me the best can be my date Friday night."

All the girls from the circle started to rush him, so he shouted, "One at a time please! You all will get a chance to show me what you got."

Shaniquia was the first one to kiss Allen. She grabbed him by the back of his head and yanked him to her mouth. She practically shoved her tongue down his throat, making him pull away out of discomfort.

"Next!" he shouted. Mariah came up to Allen and laid one on him. She bit his lip before she went in for the kiss. After they were done, Allen touched his lip in pain as he watched her walk back into the midst of the gang of girls.

"Next contestant," Allen said.

Victoria began walking back up to Allen, and right when she was about to grab his face for the kiss, Carmen came through the group of waiting females and got in-between Victoria and Allen. Victoria had shock written all over her face, but before Allen could give her an apologetic look, Carmen pushed him up against the locker and started to kiss him on his neck, slowly moving her kisses to his cheek until she reached his mouth. She kissed him slow and sensually, giving Allen memories of what went down in his Chevy on Saturday. Carmen slowly pulled away from the kiss, leaving Allen there with his eyes closed, absorbing everything that went down. Carmen began to walk away, giving all the girls a "Yeah I'm The Baddest Bitch" look, but Allen grabbed her wrist, staring only at her when he said, "I found me a winner."

All the girls rolled their eyes and their necks and broke up the group right as the warning bell rang. The Clique Boys stayed by their lockers, continuing to watch what was going on.

Allen continued, "So I'll pick you up at seven?"

Carmen laughed and combed her hair out of her face with her fingers and said, "I don't want to go to the dance with you Allen. I just wanted a kiss."

Allen tissed and pulled her in closer to him, saying, "Well too bad. I'm picking you up at seven, okay?"

"Fine Allen," Carmen said, playfully rolling her eyes. She put both her hands in her tight jeans pockets and began to make her way to her second hour class.

Allen bit his lip, thinking about that sexy kiss and went to open his locker so that he could get his Civics book out.

"Did you see that?" Marcus asked Torean.

Torean nodded his head slowly, "Yeah man."

"Aye, where are you going?" Drew asked Torean when he noticed that he was walking towards Allen's locker.

"Imma teach my student a lil' lesson."

Torean walked up to Allen's locker and tapped him on the shoulder. Allen looked up and when he saw Torean, he smiled at him, saying, "What's good?"

Torean clenched his jaw and tightly said, "Meet me at my apartment tonight at seven."

Allen was trying to figure out what was wrong with Torean's demeanor. He was acting like he was pissed at him for something.

"For what man?"

But it was too late. Torean had already gathered his boys and was on their way to their classes, five minutes late.

Allen closed his locker and started walking to Civics, thinking about Carmen's powerful kiss and the random meeting he had with the Clique Boys at seven 'o clock. Though the meeting was random, he wasn't at all concerned with what it might be about; it was hard for him to worry too much at the moment.

THE CLIQUE BOYS
Thursday, 7:00pm ~ TOREAN'S APARTMENT

"HEY TOREAN, YOU WANTED TO SEE ME?"

Torean led Allen inside his apartment and directed him to sit on the couch. The Clique Boys were all standing, Torean stood in front of them, closest to Allen.

"What's with the whole serious vibe goin' on around here?" Allen could not help but notice how the lights were dim, no cell phones were ringing, and there was not a single happy-looking face in the group. Finally, Torean spoke.

"I wanted you here to talk about what's been going on with you at school."

"What about it?" Allen asked concerned.

"I mean how you've been acting since becoming a player."

Allen's face turned smug, "You know I learned from the best."

"And that's exactly what we're here for. I just wanna make it clear that I am the best." Torean said sternly.

Allen's eyes got big once he finally figured out what was goin on, "Oh, I get it. You're scared of competition."

Torean laughed, "Scared of what? Do you seriously think you're my competition?"

"I *know* I'm your competition."

"Unless you forgot Allen, we all made you and we damn sure can break you."

"Uh huh," Allen said, pulling out his cell phone, acting like this whole thing was a waste of time.

Torean got mad, "Did you hear what I just said?"

"Yeah, yeah, yeah. You made me and you can break me. Big deal."

Torean looked at his boys and gave an angry laugh before turning back to Allen, "Oh, you must think you're big shit now, comin' at me like that."

"What's your deal Torean? I'm not doing anything wrong; you're the one over here being a player hater. I'm just making a new name for myself other than Allen the Funny Man. I can't help it if I look better, dress better, and run game better than you and your boys back there."

The Clique Boys inched closer to Allen. Torean moved even closer, wanting to give him the full effect of his intimidation.

"But the thing is Allen, I run Wilson High. I'm the best dressed, best looking, best ladies' man, and the best player Wilson has seen since Drew's brother graduated from this school. Ain't no way in hell I'm gonna have some player-for-a-day tell me this bull."

Allen stood up, "As you can see, I'm a player 'till the end. Once a player, always a player. And once Allen gets on the scene, Torean needs to watch his back."

"Why do I need to watch my back?"

Allen just smiled, "'Cause I'm about to steal that crown you rockin'."

"Do you honestly think that you're a better player than me?"

"I *know* that I'm a better player than you," Allen boldly said. He couldn't believe that his so-called friends brought him here for drama. But he definitely was not about to back down from anyone, not even the Clique Boys.

Torean paced his living room back and forth in silence. Finally after what seemed like ten minutes, Torean looked up at Allen, "Okay, let's settle this whole thing. How about we see who's the biggest player at this school once and for all? I propose that whoever can get one of the baddest girls at Wilson to say 'I love you' first will become the major player at Wilson High."

Allen raised his eyebrows skeptically, "Are you serious?"

Torean nodded his head yes. The remainder Clique Boys all looked at each other. They couldn't believe that Torean thought Allen was becoming such competition that he had to resort to that.

"Alright then. You got yourself a challenge," Allen answered Torean and they both exchanged a handshake. Allen left Holloway Apartments and looked through his contacts for the perfect girl. He knew exactly who he wanted to call.

Once all was clear from Allen, the Clique Boys bombarded Torean with questions.

"Why would you make a bet like that with Allen?"

"Is it really that serious Torean?"

"Why didn't we beat him up?"

He put his hand up to silence them before he spoke.

"Look, Al's no competition here. He never had a girlfriend, let alone someone who will fall in love with him. Me on the other hand, knows exactly who I want, and how I'm gonna get her to fall in love with me."

Torean said all this with such confidence that the Boys had no choice but to believe him. He was the leader of the most popular group at school. And Allen? He was just the class clown.

The game was on.

ALLEN RIVERA
Sunday, 5:34p.m. ~ LIVING ROOM

"HEY ALLEN, YOU WANNA COME IN HERE for a second?" Allen's dad asked him from the living room. Allen strode from the kitchen, checking to see what his dad wanted.

"Padre?" Allen said to his dad.

His dad patted the empty seat on the couch, "Come have a seat with me son. I feel like I haven't talked with you in a very long time."

Allen plopped down on the couch and watched the pre game for the Packers with his dad. His father cleared his throat and Allen prepared himself for whatever it was that his dad wanted to say to him.

"How has school been going for you? I'm happy to hear that you haven't received any bad reports lately."

Allen replied, "School has been fine. Nothing too exciting has been going on," he lied.

Allen's father rubbed the stubble on his chin, "Is that right?" he quietly said. Allen stared at the television once more.

His dad began to speak again, "I think something has been going on with you lately. There have been a lot of young ladies running in and out of my house these past few weeks," Allen's dad looked at him for an answer.

Allen shook his head and softly laughed, "They're just girls, dad. I'm not interested in them like that."

"Well you're inviting them over; don't you think that maybe they believe you feel differently?"

Allen opened his mouth to speak, but couldn't think of anything to say.

"Look son, I'm not going to jump to conclusions here; maybe they really are just your friends," Allen's dad leaned in closer to Allen, "But if all of these girls are doing more than just playing UNO with you, I just want you to make sure that you're being careful."

"Dad!" Allen groaned in embarrassment.

His father continued, "Sex is a very serious subject Allen. It is something that should only be shared between two people who are committed, really care about one another, and are mentally ready for such a huge step. I would be very disappointed in you if you were to be sleeping around with all these girls and know in your heart that they don't mean a thing to you. Girls are emotional creatures and sleeping with them and then deciding to treat them like they do not exist the next day can do serious damage to their self-esteem."

Allen buried his head in his hands in embarrassment, "Dad, it's not even like that."

"Well what is it like then?"

"We're just fooling around. It's nothing serious," Allen honestly answered.

"We're just fooling around? It's nothing serious?" his dad said, "What about when this fooling around escalates to something more? What about if something serious does happen? STDs are very serious Allen and they can certainly come from 'just fooling around'," Allen's father shook his head at his son, "The last thing I want you to think is that just because you are not having sex with anyone *yet*, that sexually transmitted diseases cannot occur."

"I understand Dad."

"Just think about this: if all these girls that you have been messing around with have been so easy to hook up with you, then they definitely have not hesitated to fool around, maybe even have sex, with other people as well," he seriously said, "What if they're hopping around, guy to guy, not knowing that they have anything? And then they come to you and pass their disease right along,"

"Papá, espera un segundo," Allen gently put his hand up to pause his father, "I am not having sex dad. I don't plan to have sex with anyone until I meet the right person, and right now, these chicks that have come over here are not who I want. I'm popular now and stuff like this only comes with the territory. I am not trying to sound like a douche," Allen could see that his dad was not favoring his words at this point, "but I just want to be honest with you. If the time comes where I decide to have sex with someone, I will definitely make sure that I use protection."

"Heck, I know you better! I'm not trying to see you on *Sixteen and Pregnant*."

Allen laughed, "I don't want to see me on that show either, Dad."

"So then you need to make sure that you're being responsible. And more importantly," his dad said, "you need to make sure that you treat these women out here with respect."

Allen nodded his head and his father gave him a pat on the back, "Well, that was easy," his dad joked, "I thought I was going to have to bring your mom in here for support."

"Trust me, that's the last thing I would have wanted," Allen replied, getting scared just from the thought of listening to his mom preach about abstinence.

His dad chuckled, "Of course not Son," he then turned the volume up on the television, "Now, you ready to see the Packers murder these Bears?"

"What? The Bears will kill those cheese heads!"

Allen's dad put on his serious face, "You willing to bet on it?"

Allen put his hand out for a handshake, "You're on old man."

Allen loved listening to his father give him advice. He knew that everything his dad said came from experience. Allen was just a bit disappointed in himself that he had already disrespected some females before his dad got the chance to stop him. Even worse, there wasn't a way Allen could stop himself from using girls, especially with the bet going on. At the end of the day, he *had* to use someone. He knew that this girl did not deserve to be treated that way, but he was not about to back down from Torean for anyone or anything.

NEISHA THOMPSON & TOREAN HUDSON
Monday, 1:20p.m. ~ SOPHOMORE HALLWAY

Neisha walked down the hall with her head
held high and her Prada bag hanging on her arm. Mac lip gloss
on and Beyonce's Heat perfume lingering everywhere she
walked past. She caught the stares of every boy standing
around the hallway. One thing she hated about walking down
the hall was passing by the Clique Boys' lockers and how she
could not avoid them no matter how hard she tried. It would
not bother her so much if one of those Clique Boys were not
Marcus Hamilton. Being around him made her awkward. The
past they shared was still too fresh for her to get over and
every time she saw his face, a status update on Facebook, or
even a tweet on Twitter, all of the memories and emotions
rushed at her like it all happened just yesterday. Neisha had
such a huge crush on Marcus and he took advantage of her
feelings when he tried to use her for sex. Even though they did
not sleep together, Neisha felt so stupid that she actually
considered having sex with Marcus because she thought he
actually had sincere feelings for her. But in the end, Neisha
found out that he was hooking up with another girl behind her
back the entire time.

She tried her hardest to keep her eyes forward while she
began to walk near the four lockers. Though her palms began
to sweat, she inconspicuously wiped them on her jeans and
kept strutting her stuff down the hallway.

Torean watched her with curious eyes. Anytime he saw Bryanna walking without Neisha or Neisha without Bryanna, he always had to take advantage of the situation. And this time would be no different.

"Hey," Torean smoothly said to Neisha, who just made her way up to the boys. Luckily for her, only Torean and Marcus were there.

Neisha cursed in her head, but stopped and gave Torean a fake smile, "Hey Torean."

"What's up Neisha?" said Marcus. He gazed at Neisha with lustful eyes, taking a while to reach her face from staring at every other part of her body. Neisha decided to ignore his greeting and walked off again. Marcus mischievously chuckled to himself.

"Where you goin'? I wasn't done talkin' to you," Torean said.

She cocked her head at him, "Well *excuse* me Mr. Hudson. I didn't know you were running things like that."

"Where your girl at?" Torean asked while he slowly gazed at another girl's butt.

"Bryanna is talking to our cheerleading coach about something. Why don't you just text her and see what's up?" Neisha hurriedly replied, wanting to get away from Marcus Hamilton as soon as possible before her hands turned into a sweaty disaster.

"What you in a rush for?" Marcus stared, his usual cocky snide on his face.

Neisha looked at him and nonchalantly shrugged her shoulders.

Marcus stepped up to her and rubbed his golden brown hand up and down the sleeve of her cardigan, "Why you bein' so quiet, ma?"

Neisha stood there in silence, but didn't move her arm away from his touch.

"You look good today," Marcus continued. His Axe smelled intoxicating and his voice had her in a trance, just like always. But also just like always, thoughts of how much he humiliated her pushed themselves to the forefront of her brain and caused her to snap out of her daze.

"Just text her," Neisha quickly snapped to Torean before leaving the two handsome boys.

Torean tapped Marcus and then moved his head in her direction, "What was that all about?"

Marcus chuckled, "I just had to let her know that I could still have her if I wanted her. You saw the way she was caught up in me, right?"

"Yeah I peeped that."

"Neisha and I both know Trent is just a distraction to keep her away from me."

Torean's eyebrows came together curiously, "And what is Lynda to you?"

Marcus rolled his eyes, "Besides being annoying, Lynda is here to make Neisha miserable. Every chance Lynda gets, she will rub in Neisha's face that she got me in the end."

"What makes you think Lynda is rubbing anything in Neisha's face? And why do you think that Neisha is miserable?" Torean asked, looking at another butt that passed by.

Marcus stared at the same backside before he answered, "Lynda Andrews has always been a bragger and this is something everyone knows, including me. That's the only reason I'm still with her," he cockily laughed, "and the fact that her head game is amazing."

Torean gave his boy a play.

"And as far as Neisha goes," Marcus continued, "She wanted me so bad. You remember how she was. There's no way in the world she can see me and Lynda together without being jealous."

Torean pulled out his EVO, "Man you put too much thought into this stuff," he said to his best friend, "If you want the girl back, that's all you had to say."

"Man, ain't nobody thinking about her," Marcus replied rudely. He noticed Torean gathering up his books.

"What you 'bout to do?" He asked.

Torean smiled despite himself, "I'm about to see what Bryanna's up to. I have a bet to win, remember?"

"Alright, I'll catch you later then," Marcus and Torean gave each other a dap before Torean headed off to find Bryanna. While walking, all Torean could think about was how he did not want to end up like his boy Marcus. After Marcus got done playing with a girl's heart, he ended up getting the short end of the stick, and Torean did not want to end up looking stupid when this bet was over and done with.

TOREAN HUDSON & ALLEN RIVERA
Monday, 3:17pm PARKING LOT

Torean walked out of the school, closely followed by his Clique Boys.

"Hold up. Let me holler at Al for a sec," Torean walked over to Allen, who was leaning against his truck, talking to Patrick.

"Like I was saying," Patrick said, "you can never ask a girl if she's wearing a weave; they get way too defensive about those types of things."

Allen looked up at Torean when he came by the Chevy.

"What's up?" he said to Torean.

The two of them exchanged a dap while Torean looked over at Patrick, wondering what he was still doing there.

"I'll get at you later Al," Pat said to his best-friend-half-of-the-time, before walking towards his car.

Once Patrick was gone, Torean got ready to discuss business.

"So, Mr.Wanna-Be Major Player at Wilson,"

Allen laughed.

"Did you find your girl yet?" he finished.

Allen nodded his head smoothly, "Yeah, I'm rolling with Carmen," Torean already knew he was going to say that, so he wasn't surprised at all.

"What about you?" Allen asked.

Torean licked his lips suavely, and he said, "It's Bryanna."

"Word?" Allen asked, genuinely taken aback.

"Yeah," Torean had called up Bryanna as soon as his boys left his place the night of the bet and started running his toughest game on her. He was doing things such as telling her how beautiful she was and how he would love to spend some more time with her. Even earlier today, he threw a ton of complements her way. Of course, she acted as if she wasn't fazed by what he said, but Torean knew that she was into it. He couldn't have picked a better girl for this bet.

"Alright, so what do we do now?"

Torean laughed, "I forgot that you've never dated a girl."

Allen rolled his eyes. He was not in the mood for Torean to state the obvious at the moment.

"Now, we take them out until we feel comfortable enough to ask them to be our girls."

"Comfortable?"

Torean explained, "It's all about comfort ability. If you don't think you're ready to get into a relationship with a girl, then you can end up dating a total zero."

"But Carmen's sexy," Allen said matter-of-factly.

Torean shook his head, "Being cute is only part of it. Yeah, they might be cool in the beginning, but when you really start to see their true colors is after the honeymoon-stage."

Allen thought back to what Torean told him about the honeymoon-stage back when he was learning the ropes on how to be a player. The honeymoon stage was when the girl started off sweet, cute, and flirtatious. But after a period of time, anywhere between the first three months of dating, either two things can happen. Either they prove that the 'sweet-n-sexy' thing is really their personality, or the guy would find out that they are a total bitch.

"So what we should do to speed along this process," Torean continued, "Is take our girls to the Wilson versus Brown game this Friday."

"A double date?" Allen said skeptically.

"It's not really gonna be a double date. It'll be more like two players goin' to the same game with two of the finest chicks at school. I don't plan to sit by you, and hopefully your ugly butt doesn't try to come near me either," Torean said to Allen.

Allen closed his eyes for a brief moment, trying to fight the urge to roast Torean on the spot for that diss. "Cool. Cool," Allen said instead, wrapping up the conversation by opening the door to his Chevy.

"Aight man, I'll see you later," Torean said, catching the hint that Allen was trying to end their conversation rather quickly.

Allen finished with, "Big ups to all my haters!" trying to be funny by quoting the lyrics to Young Dro's "Ain't I."

Torean laughed dryly, "You're hilarious man!"

"I'll be even funnier when I become the new Major Player at school!"

"Whatever!" Torean shouted to Allen, throwing up the deuces before going back to his friends. Torean was not one to hold major hostility towards a person, so he did not consider Allen Rivera to be his enemy. Plain and simple, Torean saw Allen as a bit of friendly competition. Now, if Allen ended up winning this bet, which Torean was confident he would not, their friendship just might have to take a turn for the worst.

ALLEN RIVERA
Thursday, 7:00p.m. ~ HOME

"You would be the only dork to actually show up on time for something," Allen smartly said to his best friend, Patrick.

"Shut up!" Patrick playfully punched Allen on the shoulder. Allen pretended to be hurt and crawled into the kitchen where his mom was putting out a tray of sugar cookies for the two boys.

Rosalie's face brightened when she saw Patrick, "Hola Patrick! It has been forever!"

"Hey there Mrs. Rivera," Patrick politely said. Allen's mother rushed over to Patrick and planted a kiss on both his cheeks, "Well, I'm going to let you boys have your fun. Juice is in the fridge. Bye now."

Patrick chuckled lightly while Allen's mother left the kitchen, "Dude I'm telling you; your mom wants me."

Allen threw a cookie at him. Patrick caught it and stuffed it in his mouth. Allen shook his head at his friend while he opened his laptop and went on Facebook.

"Man, some of these people have no lives," Patrick said when he saw a status about what someone planned to wear to school tomorrow.

Allen laughed as he took a bite of another cookie, "I don't know who to feel sorrier for, the people who make the statuses or people like us who spend all our free time reading them."

"Look at this," Patrick roughly pressed his finger on the screen of the laptop. Allen gave him an angry glare before looking at a new photo by Tiffany Rodgers.

"Whoa!" Allen breathed. He and Patrick looked at the picture that was just uploaded ten seconds ago, but already had thirty-four likes and sixteen comments. The photo was of Tiffany, Lauren, and Carmen, all in their bathing suits at Lauren's indoor swimming pool. Each of the girls' breasts looked like they were ready to pop out of their skimpy tops, and they made it even more seductive by doing a sexy pose by the pool.

"These girls definitely know how to drive the fellas crazy," Patrick said daze-like. "If I were you, I would hate to see my girl showing her body off like that for all the boys to see."

"Well she's not my girl yet," Allen replied, nonetheless getting bothered by what the people were commenting on their picture.

"So how does it feel?" Patrick randomly said.

Allen looked at him confused, "How does what feel?"

"Being so popular with the ladies. I mean, I play sports and all, but I have no time for a girl in my life right now, so I just want to know how it feels."

Allen thought for a bit, "I guess it feels good. Having everyone want me and want to be around me is pretty darn refreshing compared to how things used to be. But at the same time, I do feel like I'm losing who I once was. Comedy was my life, but now all it seems like I have time for is hanging out."

"And that doesn't bother you?"

"I try not to let it. As long as I get Carmen, everything will be worth it."

Patrick decided to eat a cookie instead of saying what was really on his mind.

"But anyway," Allen said, "you claimed a few minutes ago that you didn't have time to be messin' with any girls, but word around the hallways is that you have been texting Lexi Grant," Allen looked at him suspiciously.

Patrick laughed, "Well, you know."

Allen threw a cookie at him, "No, I don't know. The girl has been in this town for two weeks and you just couldn't wait to be all up in her face."

"If you must know, we're just working on a project together for chemistry. Rumors at Wilson are so ridiculous." Patrick said, shaking his head.

"Mhmm," Allen replied, not believing a word his best friend said to him.

"I just found out that I'm going to be a daddy," Patrick slowly said.

"WHAT!" Allen shouted, jumping up from his chair.

Patrick laughed, "No. Look," he pointed at the computer screen, "'I just found out I'm going to be a daddy'. Blake from home ec just posted that."

"Whew! Man you had me scared for a second," Allen dramatically said.

"Well at least he had a little bit of practice with taking care of a baby in class," Patrick joked.

Allen swatted his hand at him, "Man please, if his girlfriend Tee-Tee is the one pregnant, he better call up the Maury Show."

"And why's that?"

"Because that boy is *not* the father of that baby!" Allen said, cracking up laughing.

Now it was Allen's turn to take a sugar cookie to the face. Munching on his cookie, Allen felt a bit uneasy. Though he kept telling himself that it was just a picture, Allen could not help but to be bothered that Carmen was still doing things like taking sexy pictures for attention. The whole time he had known Carmen, the T.L.C. side of her had been hidden from him. Now that he was seeing the types of things that many other people at Wilson have been seeing, it was hard for him to keep on ignoring the fact that Carmen was not as innocent as she had always seemed to appear to be. For his sake, Allen was hoping that she had changed, but that well-liked picture of her had him a little worried.

CHARMANE WHITE

TOREAN HUDSON & ALLEN RIVERA
Friday, 6:30pm
WILSON V.S. BROWN BASKETBALL GAME

The Wilson versus Brown game started
with Brown High School in the lead. All the Wilson High
supporters were shouting at the team captain, Chris Bennett, to
pass the ball to Trent Matthews so that he could shoot the ball
and gain the lead by one point.

"Pass the ball!" Carmen shouted urgently to Chris. Allen
looked over at Carmen and smiled. He put this arm around her
shoulder and said, "Good team spirit, C!"

Carmen, Torean, and he were standing on the bleachers
closest to the court. Bryanna was cheering and standing only a
few feet away from the three. She turned her head around and
smiled at Torean. He waved coolly and winked at her,
checking out her long, brown legs before she turned back
around to pay attention to the game. After the game calmed
down a little bit, Allen began to strike up a conversation with
Carmen.

"Are you enjoying yourself?"

Carmen nodded her head enthusiastically and smiled,
"Yeah, this sport actually has some fun points to it," and then
she smiled coyly, "I also think I like it so much because I'm
with you."

"Aww," Allen said jokingly. He quickly gave her a soft
kiss on her juicy lips before saying, "You should be down
there with those cheerleaders 'cause you look so good."

PLAYER *133* HATER

Carmen rolled her eyes at the ten girls on the floor, completely switching up her mood, and said, "Boy please. Why would I possibly want to be down there with those *things*?"

Torean quickly averted his attention away from the Rhianna look-a-like cheerleader, and looked at Carmen with a weird look.

"Well one of those *things* you rollin' your eyes at happens to be my girl," he said smartly.

Allen swatted his hand at Torean, "She ain't yo' girl yet man."

"Man, did it look like I was talkin' to you?"

"Guys, it really isn't that serious," Carmen told the two, "Sorry Torean," she said politely, "I wasn't talking about Bryanna, I was directing that comment towards Victoria."

Allen raised his eyebrows, "What's wrong with Vicky?"

Carmen looked over at him and said, "She keeps trying to get at you even though she knows I called dibs."

Allen gave her another kiss just for being so cute. Torean rolled his eyes at the scene taking place, wishing that it could be him and Bryanna kissing all over each other instead.

Finally, the half-time show started, and the Golden Lion's mascot was running out to the Rej3cts hit song "Cat Daddy". Everyone cheered on the mascot while he did the popular dance. Even the cheerleaders joined in. Once the song was over, the Golden Lion began to shout one of his crowd chants to get everyone pumped up for the second half of the game.

Who's that rockin' that blue and gold?
Wilson, that's us!
Whose lion gets down on the floor?
Wilson, that's us!

Who's that whoopin' that other team? Who's that rockin' it hard on the scene?

Wilson!

Who?

Wilson!

Who?

WILSON, WILSON, WILSON!

The remainder of the game went by in a breeze. Allen and Carmen continued to flirt with each other, and Torean continued watching Bryanna's every movement as she had cheer sex with him. Bryanna looked good enough to eat, and Torean didn't mind doing that.

Brown kept creeping up on the scoreboard and Wilson continued to give it all they had. The ballers kept ballin', the cheerleaders kept cheerin', and the supporters kept supportin'. The game was so close that the intensity could be felt all over the gym.

The game was tied 78 to 78 at the last minute. Wilson was in position with the ball and Chris has passed it to the sophomore, Cordell. He dribbled the ball down the court and passed it to Trent. The ball was intercepted by the Brown players, but Chris got it back in the last ten seconds. Chris shot the ball, and what seemed like slow motion, the ball made it into the basket right as the buzzer went off.

Everyone rushed out of the bleachers and onto the floor where they bombarded the players. Torean rushed right towards Bryanna who was packing up her things. He grabbed her face and gave her a strong kiss.

"I've wanted to do that all night," he said romantically once he pulled away from her lips.

Bryanna looked around her, and noticed that everyone was watching them. He literally took her breath away, and she enjoyed every second of it. Torean noticed that Allen was also staring at them, so in return, he gave Allen a cocky look, *That's how it's done!*

Torean, Bryanna, Carmen, and Allen all walked out of the school and into the crowded parking lot. Torean's arm was lightly wrapped around Bryanna's shoulders, and Allen did the same. Still irritated at Torean's smooth kiss a bit earlier, Allen stopped in mid-stride, not wanting Torean to one-up him on his date. He winked at Torean, grabbed both of Carmen's dainty hands, and said, "Carmen, you know that I'm feelin' you right?"

Carmen nodded her head easily and said, "Yeah."

Torean rolled his eyes. He already knew what Allen was about to do, and Torean definitely didn't want the class clown to beat him to it.

"And you're feeling me, aren't you?" Allen continued, looking Carmen right in her brown eyes.

Torean wrapped his arm around Bryanna's shoulder a little more tightly and smoothly whispered into her ear, "I wanna be with you," he said every word slowly so that Bryanna could let his words sink in. They walked a few feet away from where Allen stood with Carmen, so that he could run his award-winning game in private.

Bryanna rolled her eyes, "I already know you want to have sex with me Torean."

Torean laughed quietly in her ear, making her tickle, "No, I mean I wanna be with you. In a relationship."

Bryanna paused.

Allen continued, "So if two people are feelin' each other on the same level, and did the things that me and you did, don't you think we should make it official by going out with each other?"

"So what do you think? You wanna give this player a chance by being my girl?" Torean asked her, adding more want-ability in his already persuasive voice.

Bryanna looked Torean in his grey eyes and said, "Are you being serious Torean? Like *really* being serious?" she squinted her eyes up at him, hoping to catch some sort of sign that he was being insincere.

He kissed her cheek reassuringly, saying, "I've wanted to be with you since Marcus' party. I'm attracted to everything about you. I want us to be together. And I hope you wanna be with me too."

"Yes or no Carmen, I'm dying out here!" Allen playfully begged her, looking anxiously over at where Torean was all hugged up with Bryanna, most likely having the same conversation that he was.

Carmen reached her head up and gave Allen one of the best kisses he's ever had, and shouted back at him, "Yes! Yes, I'll go out with you."

"I wanna be with you Torean, but I just don't know," Bryanna looked down at the ground when she spoke, too afraid to look up at Torean because she finally admitted something she has tried to deny for a very long time.

"If you wanna be with me, then just say yes," Torean whispered to her.

"Well then, I want to be with you," Bryanna answered to Torean, biting her lip down nervously.

Without speaking to Torean, Allen led his new girlfriend to his Chevy to take her home. Carmen was so happy that Allen had finally asked her out. She has been waiting for this moment ever since he became so cool. Allen was the perfect guy for her, and she couldn't wait to see how this relationship went.

Torean noticed that Allen was leaving, so he picked up Bryanna's cheer bag, and the two of them strolled over to his Mercedes.

Bryanna genuinely wanted to say yes, but she couldn't help but wonder why all of a sudden Torean wanted to ask her out. She had never said yes to anyone at all who asked her out, and it was a known fact that Torean Hudson did not ask just anyone to be his girlfriend. Bryanna had known that she should have been elated about that, but it was going to take some time to get used to the whole relationship thing.

Torean did not like how unsure Bryanna was acting. He thought she would jump at the chance to be his girl; any other girl would have. After tonight, seeing Bryanna in her element and watching her expression after he kissed her, Torean was quickly learning that Bryanna was not like any other girl at Wilson High School.

CHARMANE WHITE

TOREAN HUDSON & BRYANNA WILLIAMS
Friday, 8:00 pm ~TOREAN'S APARTMENT

"Okay, okay, you win!" whined Bryanna.
She fought her way up from under Torean, still giggling from
the tickling she just endured. The couple was hanging out in
Torean's apartment watching scary movies.

Torean playfully brought Bryanna back down onto the
ground, laying over her, "You sure you don't want a round
two?" he flirtatiously asked her, his lip lightly bit as he stared
down at her beauty.

"Positive," Bryanna replied. The last thing she wanted was
for Torean's grandmother to catch the two of them rolling
around on the floor like horny teenagers.

Torean propped himself up and sat on the floor against the
couch; Bryanna did the same. He wrapped his arm around his
girlfriend, pulling her in close to him. Bryanna enjoyed being
this intimate with him; it was something she looked forward to
just about every night. One thing that Bryanna could for sure
say was that the two of them had come a very long way since
she got fingered by Torean in Marcus' kitchen. Torean was
her official man now, and things were going great. While she
used to walk around Wilson like a queen, Bryanna now
strutted down the halls like a goddess, and Torean had every
bit to do with it. Being with a Clique Boy took Bryanna's
social status to a whole other level. Bryanna loved the perks

that came with dating Torean Hudson, but most importantly of all, she simply loved just being with him.

"You know," Bryanna whispered in Torean's ear, "If you're only tickling me to avoid watching this movie, we can just put in a Disney flick or something."

Torean chuckled, "I might just have to take you up on that offer," Guts and gore was not something Torean enjoyed to watch for two hours. He only put up with it because Bryanna was always talking about how much she loved horror movies. Being such a considerate boyfriend was a lot of hard work for Torean, but he was starting to get used to it. Torean took his girlfriend out on expensive dates every weekend, called her throughout the day just to say hello, and he even bought Bryanna a Tiffany's charm bracelet that she rocks on her wrist every day. Torean knew that he was doing a great job at charming Bryanna, and he felt very confident that she was falling for him. They had been dating for three weeks now; falling for Torean this far in the game was unavoidable.

Bryanna cared for Torean. Everything he did pointed to the fact that he made such a good catch, but at the same time, Bryanna could not help but to have her doubts. She believed that no matter how pretty and popular she may have been, Torean didn't date *anyone*, and now that he was dating her, she couldn't help but be suspicious of his motives. The last thing she wanted was to be just another girl on the list of females Torean Hudson had played and manipulated.

Torean was feeling good about choosing Bryanna to be his bet-girl. So far, every day that they had spent together had made him happy and confident that Bryanna was sure to fall in love with him. In Torean's eyes, Torean and Bryanna were like the high school Will and Jada Smith, while Allen and Carmen were like Justin Beiber and Selena Gomez. With the amount of expertise he had, Torean just knew that he had the bet in the bag. Allen had absolutely nothing on him.

ALLEN RIVERA & CARMEN SANCHEZ
Friday, 8:00 pm ~ LUCKY LANES

At the Lucky Lanes Bowling Alley, Carmen and Allen were trying to enjoy each other's company in the black lit building. Once Allen found out that Carmen had never been bowling before, he knew that he had to take her out. As soon as their game got started though, Allen had quickly regretted letting his girlfriend anywhere near a heavy ball.

"Whoa babe, not so hard!" Allen shouted at Carmen, helplessly watching Carmen slam the bowling ball onto the floor in her attempts to knock over some pins. To his surprise, she was able to knock over six of them.

"See, I know what I'm doing," Carmen teased.

Allen playfully rolled his eyes at his girlfriends banter. Even though Allen started this whole thing off on a bet, he was really starting to get strong feelings for Carmen. It was not that he never had feelings for her before, but the way that he felt now that the two of them were a couple was something that he had never felt before.

Carmen thought that Allen was the best thing that had ever happened to her. Most of the guys she dated were ignorant, conceited, and jerks, but Allen was funny, adorable, and knew how to treat a lady. Right now, Allen was doing everything right, and that made Carmen feel so lucky. Not only was she dating one of the most popular guys at Wilson, but she was also dating one of the most caring guys that she had ever known. Just last week he gave her a basket of assorted chocolates, which definitely gained some ooo's and ahhh's from her fellow T.L.C.s. Even though Carmen saw Torean do that for his girlfriend Bryanna Wilson a few days earlier, she knew that Allen had thought of it first.

While Allen watched Carmen set up to finish knocking out her remaining pins, he thought back to how he stole Torean's idea of buying a basket of chocolates for his girl. When he saw the giddy reaction, Bryanna had after receiving her gift, Allen just had to make Carmen react that same way. The old Allen would never do anything less than original for a girl he liked, but the old Allen would not participate in such a cruel bet either. All the dates, all the hook-ups, and all the conversations that the two of them had shared were starting to make him feel guilty for what he was doing to her. There was a point in time where Allen would never have pictured himself doing this to the girl of his dreams. But Allen couldn't forget that he was a player now and that he had to stick to the rules. He hoped Carmen could understand that. Better yet, Allen hoped she never had to find out.

Carmen jumped up and down in celebration for knocking over the rest of her pins. Wiggling her hips as she walked over to Allen, who was sitting in a chair, she gave him a big smooch on his lips.

"I need to take you bowling more often," Allen flirtatiously joked.

Carmen winked at him before taking her seat so that Allen could take his turn. It had been three weeks since their relationship had become official, and Carmen had noticed that Allen hadn't pressured her into having sex with him like those other players she had messed around with had done. Carmen absolutely appreciated that about Allen. Whenever she was with him, Carmen felt so carefree. With Allen, Carmen did not feel the need to rush into something that she was not ready to do. Carmen knew that Allen had been patiently waiting for her to show him how much she cared for him, and she was ready to take things to the next level. Carmen wanted to do something to thank Allen for being such a great boyfriend to her. Something only a T.L.C. knew how to do best.

ALLEN RIVERA
Sunday, 9:00am ~ CATHOLIC MEMORIAL CHURCH

"Today, congregation, we will be learning about the act of forgiveness."

"Blah, blah, blah," Allen mumbled to himself. Though he did like going to church, he was unbearably tired today and all he wanted to do was close his eyes and go to sleep. His life would be so much easier if service did not start until two o'clock. That would at least give him the proper eight hours of sleep he needed to be able to concentrate on what his pastor was saying.

Allen slowly let his head drift towards the back of the uncomfortable, wooden pew, and his mom slapped him on the leg.

"Pay attention hijo!" she whispered to him. Allen woke up quickly, hearing the sound of a girl snickering. He turned his head around and saw that the laughter was coming from his girlfriend, Carmen. Allen smiled at her and she waved, then Mrs. Rivera smacked Allen upside the head to get him to pay attention.

The sermon slowly dragged on and Allen tried to do whatever he could to stay awake. He tried reciting the lyrics to "Say Goodbye" by Chris Brown. He chewed on some Spearmint to keep him occupied, even though all that did was make him hungry. He could already tell that this was going to be the longest three hours he had ever had to sit through in his life.

"Mom, I'll be right back," Allen heard Carmen say from behind him. He was surprised because Carmen never got up to leave service, not even to go to the bathroom. Which, now that Allen thought about it, he needed to use the restroom too.

Allen stood up slowly and made his way towards the bottom level of the church where the bathrooms were located. When he walked down the last few steps, he saw Carmen standing at the landing, looking like a pin-up for Playboy Magazine. With her good-girl looking white dress, and the look of pure lust on her face, she would've been perfect for a Catholic Girl Gone Wild movie. Carmen continued to stay leaned up against the wall, and biting her lip, "It's about time you came down here."

Allen looked at her curiously, "I guess it was just a coincidence."

Carmen licked her lips seductively, "No baby. There aren't coincidences. I wanted you to follow me and you did."

Allen smiled at her, "I guess I did."

She began to walk up to Allen, and with every step she took, she started to take her clothes off slowly, not caring that she was undressing in the middle of the hallway. Allen's heart began to pound in his chest.

"Now, you've been real good to me Allen. Real good. And now I just want to do something real good to you," Carmen sexily said to Allen, slowly undoing her dress.

Allen looked around his surroundings, and his eyes got big, "In church?"

Carmen let her dress fall to the floor, revealing her white lingerie that barely covered her curvy body. She walked right up to Allen, pushing him against the wall and whispered in his ear, "It's okay. God will forgive us."

Allen's arousal got the best of him and Carmen smiled at his bulging pants. He wanted to have sex with her so bad. But in church? That took sinning to a whole other level...*Oh well.*

The two of them began to kiss each other passionately while Carmen allowed Allen to feel all over her body. Carmen quickly pulled away, giving Allen a sneaky look, "I wanna play a game."

"What kinda game?" Allen asked, trying to kiss her on her neck.

"How about you be the pastor, I'll be the sinner, and *this* can be a confessional." Carmen said, pointing to the closet across from the bathroom.

"We. Can. Do. Whatever. You. Want," Allen replied, kissing her with every word he spoke.

Carmen bit her lower lip and began pulling him by his tie.

"Well then, come with me pastor. I've been a very naughty girl."

***

Allen walked back into service looking disheveled. His shirt wasn't tucked in, his belt was halfway done, and his tie was loose.

"Where have you been?" Rosalie shout-whispered to Allen.

"Nowhere ma. Just to the bathroom."

Mrs. Rivera gave her son another look-over and replied, "Well you need to clean yourself up. You look like you've been up to no good."

CHARMANE WHITE

Once again, Allen heard the familiar laugh from Carmen. He turned around to look at her, sitting there looking like an angel, and she flirtatiously smiled at him before opening her Bible up.

Allen turned back around and quietly slid his cell phone out of his pocket. He looked at the clock that read 11:02a.m. and tissed. He still had to be at church for another hour. *Dammit.*

Losing his virginity to Carmen in a church closet was a crazy experience for Allen. A twinge of guilt haunted his conscience because he felt like he should have waited to have sex in a more appropriate place, like a bed for instance. At the same time, Allen could not shake the feeling of the overwhelming pleasure. What he shared with Carmen was something he was sure never to forget. Losing his virginity was powerful, pleasurable, and all so new to him. Allen could not have been happier that Carmen decided to share that experience with him.

ALLEN RIVERA & THE CLIQUE BOYS
Monday, 7:45am
SOPHMORE HALLWAY

"You did what?"

Allen modestly laughed. He stood in the Sophomore Hallway along with the Clique Boys. He just finished telling his friends, and competition about what happened with Carmen yesterday morning. All the Clique Boys had the look of both respect and envy on their handsome faces. Once Torean was able to wipe the crazy look off his face, he said, "I'm sorry man, but Carmen really let you hit? In church?"

"Yeah man. I know it sounds crazy, but everything I told you is what went down," Allen replied, looking Torean in the eyes to see his reaction.

Torean turned his head away from Allen and scratched it in thought. While thinking, Bryanna strolled over to him and wrapped her arms around his neck, giving him a hello kiss.

"Hey baby," Torean said, losing his train of thought for a second. She was super fine today. Her outfit was bangin' and her lip-gloss was poppin', and all he wanted to do was lick every little bit of her Mark Juice Gems right off her soft lips. If only Bryanna would let *him* hit. After 15 minutes in heaven with him, she would definitely have told him how much she loved him.

"What are you doing here so early?" Bryanna asked her man.

Drew laughed, "Dang girl. You over here all in his business."

She rolled her eyes.

Torean answered her, "It's no big deal Bre. Allen wanted to holler at us, so we met up a little bit early to talk."

Ricky tapped Drew on the shoulder, "And he actually answered her!"

Marcus slapped Ricky upside his head.

Bryanna ignored the immature boys, "Oh, you guys were just havin' a little Clique talk?"

Allen shook his head, "Nah, I'm not a Clique Boy."

"Well, you could've fooled me. You're always hanging around with these idiots," Bryanna playfully hit her boyfriend.

Allen laughed at Bryanna, happy that someone hit Torean, no matter how soft it might have been.

At the weak tap Bryanna gave him, a light bulb in Torean's gorgeous head went off. The nervousness that he felt when Allen told him about having sex with Carmen went away.

Now, a devious smile crept on his face and he began to feel really Clique Boy-like. He definitely had a new game plan.

"You, you, and you, come with me," Torean said to Drew, Ricky, and Marcus, "And you," he said to Allen, "meet me at my house at the usual time."

All four of the Clique Boys left Allen and Bryanna standing in the hall, while they walked into the boy's bathroom in a hurry, yet coolly at the same time. It seriously reeked of urine and weed, but they had to go somewhere to talk.

"So what's up?" Marcus asked his best friend.

Torean mischievously smiled at his friends and said, "I know exactly what we need to do to get this guy to mess up the bet."

"What?" they all asked.

Torean chuckled, "Alright, alright. Let me explain."

As the two watched the Clique Boys walk off, Bryanna curiously asked Allen, "What was that about?"

Allen shook his head, "I don't know. All I know is that I have to be at your man's house at seven."

Bryanna smiled and patted Allen on his shoulder and said, "Good luck," before walking away from him.

Allen shook his head and went to go look for his girlfriend.

Not this again. Allen was not in the mood for another one of Torean's jealousy-driven stunts today.

CHARMANE WHITE

LAFONDA RICE
Monday, 8:00a.m. ~ THE GIRL'S BATHROOM

Lafonda stood in the girls bathroom before she went off to class. Checking her make up in her cell phone screen, instead of the mirrors hanging on the wall, she double-checked to make sure she looked cute. Fuchsia lipstick, check; cheetah print press-on eye shadow, check; ponytail tacked with gel, check, basketball shorts with black stilettos and a neon orange turtle neck, check.

"Mmm mmm mmm, I look gewd!" Lafonda said to herself. She pouted her lips in the mirror and began to sing, "All eyes on may when I wawk in. No queshon dat dis girl's ah ten. Down't hate may cuz I'm brutiful!"

"Ooh, that's my song!" Tiffany shouted when she walked into the bathroom, shaking her barely covered butt off beat to the song by Keri Hilson. Lauren laughed and Carmen rolled her eyes playfully at her friend, "Tiffany, according to you, every record that comes out is your song."

Tiffany blew a big bubble with her gum and then popped it with her teeth, rolling her neck and flying her finger around, "Girl, don't start with me this early in the morning."

The whole time the T.L.Cs where conversing, Lafonda stood in her mirror, gripping the sink with all the strength she had. Luckily, Carmen did not have any classes with Lafonda, and she had not encountered her in the hallway since her and Allen had been dating. But since Lafonda finally had her in a room, she was not about to let her walk out without having a little "talk."

Guuuh guuuh ahhh guuuh Lafonda breathed heavily by the sink.

Tiffany looked at Lafonda as if she was crazy, "Umm, is somethin' wrong with you?"

"Naw, but somethin' gon' be wrong wit yer if y'all don't get outta dis bathroom right now!"

The T.L.Cs hurriedly made their way to the door, wanting to get as far away from Lafonda Rice as possible. Tiffany ran out with Lauren right at her heels. Carmen briskly followed behind them, but Lafonda closed the door right in her face.

"What are you doing?" Carmen fearfully asked.

A menacing grin appeared on Lafonda's face as she locked the bathroom door. Carmen did not know what to be more afraid of, Lafonda locking her in the bathroom, or the poor dental hygiene she had.

"I've been dreamin' ov da day when I would be abol to get yer alown," Lafonda started. She moved closer to Carmen, and Carmen cautiously walked backwards, not once taking her eyes off Lafonda as she retreated from her. Lafonda backed her into a wall and began again, "Look at yer aw scurred," she teased.

"What do you want? I haven't done anything to you!" Carmen shouted. She pulled out her phone, preparing herself to call the police. Lafonda snatched the phone with her big hands and put it in Carmen's face.

"*This* is what you've done to me!" Lafonda shouted, so angry that her words were normal.

Carmen closed her eyes when she cringed in fear from Lafonda shouting at her. But when she slowly reopened them, her eyes peered at her screensaver, a photo of her and Allen kissing each other.

"What does my boyfriend and I have to do with you?"

Lafonda was trying her hardest to calm down, but it was not working.

Guuuh guuuh ahhh guuuh

"What does Allen have to do with me? WHAT DOES ALLEN HAVE TO DO WITH ME!" Lafonda pulled out a Big Texas from her bra and stuffed half of it in her mouth. She breathed heavily as she consumed her comfort food. Lafonda took the other half of the pastry and put it in Carmen's face, "Eat."

Carmen shook her head and politely said, "Oh no. I'm trying to watch my figure."

"EAT!" Lafonda forcefully shouted at Carmen, stuffing the Big Texas in her face once again. Carmen quickly took the food from her and bit into it like her life depended on it.

"Michael Hadley Turner," Lafonda breathed almost in a poetic type of way. She backed up from Carmen and began to pace the bathroom floor, "I met him my freshman year at Wilson. I loved him with all my heart, and he wanted me too—he just had a difficult time with admitting it. Michael was a senior, you see, so once he graduated, I had to be strong and move on. But he would always be my first love.

During my sophomore year, a boy by the name of Joshua Martin Witt grabbed my attention. Even though he was a senior, we were in the same art class. I remember I surprised him on Valentine's Day with a crayon drawing of me and him holding hands under a tree. He loved the picture so much that he switched schools before he had the chance to graduate.

My heart was broken, and Matthew Garrett Moore was there to pick up the pieces. He was the defensive end, and star of the Wilson High football team. It was his senior year in school, and he had scouts from all over the country checking him out. I knew he loved me and wanted to take me off to college with him, but I was only a junior. I thought that making him stick around high school for at least another year, would help our relationship grow, so I stole his report card and changed all his A's to F's, making him fail the semester. That made him really angry, you see, because he needed to pass the semester in order to play college football. When he found out what I did to him, he yelled at me so much, but I knew that deep down inside he was happy that I did this for him—that I did this for us.

After he put a restraining order on me, I had no choice but to move on. A boy by the name of Alexander Frederick Hope caught my eye, so I made him my new boo. It was my senior year, but he was a junior. I know I shouldn't have fallen for a younger guy, but I couldn't help myself. He was everything I could have dreamed for, so I did what I had to do to stay with him. I stopped going to class and I succeeded in not graduating...but I failed at keeping Alexander. When next year came around, he got a new girlfriend and told me that he never wanted to see my face again. He had the nerve to call me a stalker. Can you believe that?

I had no choice but to get over him. It was my fifth year in school and I finally felt like I met someone special. Allen Miguel José Martinez Rivera, such a sweet name. I instantly fell in love with him during his freshman year. I don't know what I adored more, his curly locks, or his jokes. All I knew was that he just had to be my boo. He played hard to get during the first year, but I knew that he would give in eventually. Once again, I flunked my last year so that I could stick around here until he finally realized that I was the girl for him.

Now, in my sixth year at Wilson, I was *this* close to getting Allen," she put her thumb and pointer finger an inch apart from one another, "and then you came along and ruined everything."

Carmen looked up at Lafonda, who finally stopped pacing, "I'm sorry, I didn't know that you cared about Allen in this way."

"Allen Rivera is the love of my life. He's just blinded by you right now. But once I get rid of you, nothing will hold us back from being together," Lafonda said with a crazy look in her cheetah covered eyes.

"What do you mean?" Carmen asked, her fear coming back.

"A hee-hee, a hee-hee!" Lafonda evilly laughed, "I have the perfect plan," she looked at one of the bathroom stalls, "but right now, I really have to pee she skipped towards a stall, and Carmen took this as her opportunity to flee. She made a mad sprint towards the door and at the sound of the door being unlocked, Lafonda busted out of the bathroom, basketball shorts still around her ankles, and tried to catch up to Carmen, who was already out the door.

When Carmen came running out of the bathroom, she knocked right into her boyfriend.

"Allen! Oh, thank goodness it's you!" she held onto him like he was her savior.

Allen was surprised by her odd behavior, "What's wrong babe?"

"It's, it's," Carmen stammered. Before she could get her words out the couple heard the last voice on earth that they wanted to hear.

"Hay baybay!" Lafonda shouted, a huge grin on her face when she ran out the door, hoping to catch Carmen and pull her back inside.

"Allen, get away from her!" Carmen screamed, "She tried to hurt me in there!"

Allen's eyes got narrow when he looked at Lafonda, who tried to put on an angelic facial expression, "Did you really try to hurt my girl in there?" he asked, pointing at the girl's bathroom.

Lafonda twirled the strand of hair on top of her head while she coyly answered, "I tried tew…but I didn't got tew succeed juss yet."

Allen took Carmen and held onto her hand, "Look Lafonda, I do not want you!" he angrily said through gritted teeth, "Carmen is my girlfriend, and you are just some crazy girl who can't seem to take a hint. Don't you ever come near my girlfriend or me again. I don't want you!" Allen knew that his words were harsh, but he was still frustrated with the Clique Boys, and to have to deal with Lafonda Drama on top of that was just not something he felt like handling.

Lafonda stood in the hallway in shock from what Allen said. Was she really crazy? Did Allen really think Carmen Sanchez was better than she was?

"I am nawt crazay Allun," Lafonda said, "and one day yer goin' ter regret choosin' her ova may."

Allen rudely snorted at Lafonda, "Whatever," he said, turning away from her and walking his shaken up girlfriend to her locker.

Lafonda watched the retreating Allen disappear, her heart breaking with every step he took away from her.

"One day you'll regret it," she whispered, wiping a single tear from her eye. She felt the pressure of a strong hand on her upper back.

"Are you okay miss?" a deep voice said from behind her.

Lafonda turned around and rested her eyes upon her comforter.

LAFONDA RICE
Monday, 8:46a.m. ~ HALLWAY

"Are you okay?" he asked again.

Lafonda was still in shock from the handsome man who was before her. This 6'2", the bronzed skinned specimen smiled at her with teeth only the best orthodontist could produce. He had to be at least seventeen, and his faded haircut, along with the bowtie around his neck, had Lafonda drooling on the floor. Literally.

"Who yew?" Lafonda breathed.

The boy chuckled, "My name is Mitchell Tucker. I couldn't help but see what happened between you and Allen Rivera over here, and I was just coming by to make sure that everything was all right.

Lafonda got sad again at the thought of her ex boo, "I'm nowt aw right. I juss got my hawt broke," she put her head down in sorrow.

Mitchell lightly grabbed her by the chin and lifted her head up so that she was looking directly at him, "Whoa," he said. He took a long look at Lafonda's beautiful smile, though it was not perfect, he could see the sincerity and sweetness in her. Gazing at her full figure, covered by clothing that was unique and not the norm of Wilson High, he admired her differences and was infatuated by her unique appearance.

"Would you like to go out on a date with me, Lafonda?" Mitchell asked her.

"Why yew wanna go owt wit me?" Lafonda asked. No one asked her on a date before, not even her lovers. This was very surprising to her.

Mitchell softly touched the beautiful ponytail on her head, "Because a girl like you deserves to be treated like a true queen."

Lafonda touched her bra, about to pull out another Big Texas, but suddenly was not in the mood for it anymore.

"I would love to go out on a date with you," Lafonda felt as if she must have been dreaming. Never did she expect for a guy to like *her*; she was usually the one doing all the approaching. Mitchell made her feel special, something she had not felt in a long time. Lafonda hoped that he would not take that amazing feeling away from her anytime soon.

CHARMANE WHITE

THE CLIQUE BOYS
Monday, 7:03pm ~ TOREAN'S HOUSE

"Dont worry man. This is a friendly visit,
Torean said to Allen once he saw the look of apprehension on his face. Allen was nervous, no doubt because most of the time when Torean invited him over to his place, something serious happened. The first time he was transformed into a player. The next time, the bet was proposed, and now this time…He really didn't know what the Clique Boys were up to now.

"So what do y'all want then?" Allen asked the four guys.

"Take a seat. Take a seat," Torean directed to Allen. Everyone else was sitting down except Torean, so Allen sat down without hesitation.

Torean continued, "Now Allen, over a short period of time, you've been able to become a player, hook-up with the baddest girls at Wilson, become my competition, date Carmen Sanchez, have *sex* with Carmen, and I just wanna know how you did it."

Allen gave an unbelieving smile. *IS THIS BOY SERIOUS?*

"I don't know man. I guess I'm blessed," he tried to joke.

"You gotta be doin' somethin', right?" Ricky persisted.

Allen shook his head, "I'm not doin' anything that y'all ain't doin'."

Then Torean exchanged a look of enjoyment with his boys and turned back to Allen. He walked over to him and gave him an enthusiastic play, "Now that's what I wanted to hear. 'I'm not doin' nothin' that y'all ain't doin'.' That's what I'm talking about!"

Allen looked at him with pure confusion written across his face.

"This whole time I've been looking at you like you're my competition, but in fact, you're just like me," Torean said to Allen like he just had some deep revelation, "I taught you everything you know. You learned all this from a Clique Boy. And that's why I want you to be one of us."

Allen's mouth opened in shock. What? A Clique Boy? Him?

"R-r-really?" he stuttered.

"Hell yeah, really!" Torean replied, "You talk like us, dress like us, get girls like us. You're always hangin' out with our crew. Goin' to our parties, jumpin' in on our conversations; you're one of us man."

Marcus added himself in, "Allen, you're exactly what we need man. Look. I'm the man-whore of the group. Ricky's the foreigner of the group. Drew's the instigator, Torean's the leader. And you could be our funny man."

Everyone laughed at the titles Marcus gave them, and after Allen's laughter quieted down, he said, "But are you guys sure about this? I mean, this is the biggest crew in the sophomore class, and I would hate for you to mess up your reps because you added the class clown into the mix."

"When's the last time that anyone has called you the class clown?" Drew asked, "Now a day's people have been calling you one of the best players at Wilson."

"And we want the best," Ricky finished.

"So are you in?" Torean asked Allen seriously. He was looking him right in the eyes with a very intense look. Without hesitation, Allen replied, "Yeah, I'm in."

The Clique Boys all exchanged looks that Allen couldn't fully read. It seemed mischievous, but before he could make sure of it, their faces went back to their usual uninterested expressions.

Torean then said, "There's one thing that you need to do before you're initiated into the Clique Boys."

"What's that?" Allen asked.

"You have to record yourself having sex with a girl, and then bring it back to us so that we can begin the 'ceremony'," Torean answered, making air quotations at the word ceremony.

Allen knew that there was a test to initiate a guy into the Clique Boys, but never in his sixteen years of life did he think that it was this. Were they serious? Recording himself smashing a girl, then handing the tape over to Torean? That was seriously weird. But he did want in. He wanted to be in the Clique Boys as much as he wanted to have his own show on Comedy Central. Well, at least today one of those dreams would become a reality.

"Okay," Allen breathed in deeply, "I'm down."

Torean victoriously smiled to himself.

"Alright then," he said, putting hands together, "You have two days to get the job done. If you don't complete the task, then don't bother showing your face in my presence again."

Allen nodded his head, "I got you."

Torean sat down on the recliner chair and said, "You can leave now."

Allen slowly stood up and walked out the door. But before the door shut all the way, Torean stopped him, "Yo' Allen."

"Yeah?"

"Don't forget we still have a bet going on."

Allen peeked his head further in the door to look Torean in his face, "I never did."

Allen closed the door to apartment #4. He walked down the flights of steps leading outside, when his phone began to beep. He pulled out his iPhone and read the screen.

1 Missed Call
8:00pm
CarmenS.

1 New Voicemail
8:00pm
CarmenS

Allen pressed the voicemail button on his phone and a smile crept across his face when he heard her beautiful voice.

"Hi Allen, it's me Carmen. I'm just calling you because well, I needed to talk to you about some things. So just call me when you get a chance. Bye."

Allen could not wait to get home so that he could call her back. The sooner he got on the phone with her and ran some of his toughest game, the sooner he would be able to get Carmen over his house so that he could make the sex tape. Allen knew he had this challenge in the bag. Unlike Torean, Allen had already been able to sleep with his girl, so getting her to do it a second time would be a piece of cake.

TOREAN HUDSON
Wednesday, 7:13a.m. ~ APARTMENT #4

Torean walked outside of his room wearing a flannel, a pair of Hollister jeans and some fresh Jordans on his feet. Going only a few feet down the hallway, he knocked on a door that had a soft yellow sign on it, which read Stacey's Palace. After three soft taps on the door, Torean finally got an answer.

"Yes?" the sound of a young girl said from behind the door.

"You ready for school yet?" Torean asked.

"Almost."

"Aight, I'll make you something to eat," he said and then walked into the kitchen.

"Hey grandma," Torean said to the elderly lady reading her newspaper at the table. She had the same skin tone and eye color as Torean. His grandmother stuck her cheek out for a kiss that Torean sweetly gave, "Hey baby. How are you doin' today?"

Torean smiled warmly as he pulled down a box of cereal and gathered some bowls to place on the table, "I'm doing fine. I have a long day ahead of me today, so I'm just tryna get ready for that," after he poured the cereal for him and his little sister, he asked, "How are you? Did you sleep well?"

"Aw baby, I slept just fine," Torean's grandmother replied, turning the page of her paper, "And I couldn't be better hunny. Pour me some tea, will you," she added.

"Okay," as he poured a small cup of tea for his grandmother, his little sister skipped into the kitchen and eagerly began to eat her breakfast.

"Hey there little lady, you best not eat all that cereal in a hurry," said the grandmother.

Stacey giggled and then slowly began to eat her breakfast. Torean sat down at the table and looked over at his grandmother, "Gran?"

"Yes, Torean."

He hesitated for a little while before he finally asked, "So have you heard from my parents?"

Torean's grandmother, his father's mother, pretended to read the paper while she replied, "Your dad called me last night to let me know that both made it safely in Japan. He told me to tell you guys that he was happy to hear that you both were getting such good grades in school and that you've been taking such great care of the car."

"What about mommy?" Stacey asked.

"Your mom said hi too. She said that she would call you both when she gets done with work at the end of the week."

Torean tried to hide the excited grin he had on his face, but seeing the joy that his sister had as well; he just couldn't manage to cover it up. He hadn't heard from his parents in a month, mainly because his mom was a model and his dad was her, along with dozens of other models, manager. The two of them traveled all over the world taking photos and walking the runway, and that made them too busy to talk to their kids regularly. Torean and his sister had grown used to this situation over the years, but his grandmother couldn't stand the fact that her son and his wife put their careers before their children and expected for them to be fine with accepting expensive gifts every time their parents missed something. Torean knew that his parents meant the best for his little sister and him, so he did not mind the that fact that they were out living their dreams. He absolutely could not wait to hear his parent's voices finally and let them know about all the new things that had been happening in his life.

"You all done eating Stacey?" Torean asked his sister, who was now playing with the remaining bits of cereal in her bowl. She nodded her head quickly and handed the bowl for Torean to take. He grabbed the bowl from her and put it in the sink.

"Grandma, Stacey's bus is coming ten minutes late today, so you don't have to look out for it until later," he continued, "After school I'm going to pick up your church outfit before I hang out with the guys, and don't forget to call Aunt Gail and tell her happy birthday today."

"Oh my! It is her birthday, isn't it?" Torean's grandmother said in surprise. Torean chuckled at his soft-spoken grandmother while he walked into his bedroom to grab his backpack and cell phone that he never brought to the kitchen table.

"Alright guys, I'm about to go," Torean said, putting his book bag over his shoulder.

Stacey ran up to him and gave him a tight hug and a big kiss, "Bye Torean!"

"Bye bye Stacey. Be good today."

"You make sure you're good today as well young man," his grandmother told him, finally putting the newspaper down.

Torean smiled kindly at her, "I'm always good granny," his little sister Stacey and his grandmother were the only two things that kept him grounded. At Wilson, he was an overly cocky flirt, but when he was at home with his two girls, Torean was the most caring person he could possibly be.

CHARMANE WHITE

TOREAN HUDSON
Wednesday, 1:21pm ~ BIOLOGY

Two days had already passed since Torean told Allen that he wanted to initiate him into the Clique Boys. Today was the day Allen had to hand in the tape. Since nothing was in Torean's hand yet, he was getting pretty happy about the obvious outcome.

He knew the "make a sex tape" thing with Allen wasn't going to work out well; that's why he thought of it. He wanted Allen to do something stupid with a girl whom he clearly cared about, and then have him back out of it because he didn't want to hurt her. When he decided not to do the sex tape, Torean would tell everyone who was anyone about Allen not being that good of a player, turning him back into the zero that he once was and reclaim his throne as the Main Player of Wilson High. His plan was foolproof. Torean knew what kind of a person Allen was and he knew that Allen would never be able to go through with what the Clique Boys wanted him to.

"Torean, do you mind helping us out a little over here?" Neisha asked with an attitude. Torean, Drew, Bryanna, and she were all lab partners working on a human anatomy project.

"Dang girl, do you ever shut up complaining?" Torean rudely said back. Here he was minding his own business, and here this stuck-up girl goes, all up in his face as usual. If he did not know any better, he would say that Neisha might have been into him, always looking for a reason to be rude with him and roll her eyes.

Neisha said, rolling her head, "No I don't shut up. You got a problem with that?"

"Pretty much!" Drew interjected in. Bryanna threw an apple at him.

Torean and Drew exchanged a fist bump, and Torean started to help his lab partners with their project.

"That wasn't so hard, was it baby?" Bryanna said to Torean.

He quickly gave her a peck on the cheek and answered, "I'm only doing this for you," Torean was going through everything in the Player 101 manual to get this girl to fall head over heels in love with him. Just yesterday, he gave her an 'I just called because it's Tuesday' phone call and she gushed about it all day long. He was really feeling this girl and all, but he refused to let her know to what extent he cared for her. All that was important to him was getting this girl to say the three most important words. The three words that would solidify him as the king of Wilson. He just had to get Bryanna to say those words to him before Carmen said those words to Allen. What to do? What to do?

"Torean, I'm not trying to be a bitch or anything," said Neisha

Drew snorted.

"But what made you finally want to date a girl?" she finished.

Torean played with the banana in his hand that he was using for a part of their project and replied, as only Torean knew how, "I'm not just dating a girl. I'm dating a beautiful, confident woman."

"Aww!" Bryanna cooed, smiling at Torean.

He continued, saying, "I wanted to date Bryanna because she's like me in so many ways, and she's not like me in so many ways too. I think she's beautiful, sexy, and she knows how to keep me on my toes."

Drew laughed to himself. Torean definitely had a way with words.

"I've never met a girl who made me want to work for them, and when Bre came around, I just had to have her for myself."

"Well done Torean Hudson," Bryanna said, smiling appreciatively up at her boyfriend.

Torean got real close to Bryanna— Nose-to-nose close, and told her, "I meant everything I said baby."

"I know you did," she replied, grinning softly.

"Do you care about me like I care about you?" he whispered.

The words coming out of Torean's mouth was like a spell. Bryanna was being seriously caught up in his words and she wasn't ready to untangle herself just yet. She hesitated with her answer for a bit and then replied, "Of course I care about you Torean."

"Well then," Torean said to Bryanna, happy that she felt the same way for him as he did for her, "I'll be waiting for you outside the school after your practice is over. I really need to talk to you…I need to get some things off my chest."

Bryanna looked directly into his grey eyes, trying to figure out what his motives were. Torean has been nothing but sweet to her, but she did not quite fully trust him still.

"Okay, I'll see you then," Bryanna finally replied.

Torean didn't say another word about meeting up later. He didn't want to ruin the mood. Neisha and Bryanna stayed on the other side of the lab table. As Torean walked away, Neisha turned to her girl, "What does he possibly need to get off his chest?" she whispered in her friend's ear.

Bryanna shrugged her shoulders, still thinking about the look in Torean's eyes and answered, "A shirt?"

Torean knew that tonight was going to be the night. He felt that Bryanna cared about him and all he had to do was break her out of her shell and get her to be even more open with him. At that point in time, Torean believed that Bryanna no longer saw him as a player; she saw him as a genuinely good and trustworthy boyfriend.

CHARMANE WHITE

ALLEN RIVERA
Wednesday, 2:00pm ~ HOME ECONOMICS

"Mmm. This smells so good,"

Tiffany said, sniffing the aroma of their blueberry muffins.

Patrick quickly stole a muffin off the tray, making Tiffany roll her chocolate eyes at him.

"Seriously Allen, I don't know why you hang out with this kid," she half-jokingly said.

Allen laughed and replied, "This dude is my best friend for life."

"That's what I'm talkin' 'bout bro!" Patrick shouted with his mouth full with muffin while giving a high five to Allen.

"Yeah Tiffany, stop hating," Carmen joked while playing in her thick hair.

Allen jumped at the sudden vibration in his pants. He quickly pulled out his phone and read the text message from Torean:

THAT TAPE BTTR B IN MY HANDS BY 12 TONITE.

Allen blew out the air that was caught in his chest and combed his hand through his short hair. He hadn't forgotten about the initiation. He just didn't know how he was going to do it. He knew his parents were leaving to go out of town that night, so it could have been his only chance. Carmen leaned up against the counter, nibbling at a blueberry. Allen walked up to her and whispered in her ear, "You and me, tonight at my house. Eight o'clock?"

She smiled sexily at him and replied, "Sí papí."

He kissed her on her neck and gathering up his things before the bell rang.

BING!

Everyone rushed out of the classroom, and right as Allen was about to leave with Patrick to go to announcements, Carmen grabbed him by the arm, stopping him and flirtatiously said, "You and me. Seventh hour. Dressing room?"

Allen smirked, "I'll see you there."

T.L.Cs
Wednesday, 4:02p.m. ~ LAUREN'S POOL

Lauren Daniels stepfather, a tall, chubby man with a thick mustache, came over by the three girls who were coolly relaxing in the warm hot tub.

"Yes, Brian?" Lauren lazily asked when she saw him approach.

"Your mother and I have to go to the mayor's dinner tonight," Brian said in his London accent.

Lauren lazily rolled her eyes, "And?"

Carmen and Tiffany looked at each other in relaxed surprise; only Lauren would be crazy enough to get smart with her parent like that.

Brian uncomfortably cleared his throat, "*And* your mother and I just want to make sure you're going to be all right left alone for a few hours."

"Of course I'll be fine Brian," Lauren sweetly replied, giving her step dad an innocent smile, "You guys go off and have some fun."

Brian smoothed down his thick mustache while he reached into his suit pocket and pulled out his wallet. Tiffany, Lauren, and Carmen all perked up in anticipation for the wad of cash Lauren was about to get.

"Here you go gorgeous," Brian said to his stepdaughter, handing her five dollars. While Carmen and Tiffany quietly snickered, Lauren slowly took the money from him, acting as if he was giving her a dirty diaper instead of some cash.

"Th-thanks Brian," she disappointedly said to him.

"Of course Lauren," Brian replied, putting the wallet back in his pocket. He nodded his head at the three pretty girls before saying, "Well, I best be off then."

"Bye, Brian!" The T.L.Cs all shouted at his back.

"Ugh!" Lauren groaned, pushing the wisps of blonde hair away from her face, "why did my mom have to marry a cheap rich man?" she complained, looking annoyed at the innocent five-dollar bill that she held in her newly French manicured hand.

"Because he was the only person who wanted yo' momma," Tiffany mumbled to herself.

Lauren sneered at Tiffany, "You know I can hear you."

Tiffany ignored her friend and reached over the hot tub to pick up her vibrating phone, "Dang! Paul Hurst has been blowing up my phone today!" she said, looking down aggravated at her HTC.

"That sophomore from Brown High School?" Carmen asked curiously.

"Yeah," said Tiffany, in the middle of texting, "I gave him my number at the basketball game a while ago, and he has been stalking me ever since."

"Are you not interested or something?" asked Lauren.

Tiffany shrugged her shoulders, "Hell. I had to have been interested if I gave him my number, but it's like the texting never stops with him. He always has something to say or something to ask me. It seriously gets on my nerves."

"You ever think that maybe he talks to you so much because he wants to get to know you?" Carmen asked Tiffany, not understanding why she was not feeling Paul.

"Hmmm," said Tiffany, moving her eyes upward in thought, "I never thought about it that way before."

Carmen and Lauren both rolled their eyes at their best friend. Tiffany put her phone away and looked at Lauren, "Did you ever make that Top Ten list for us to post on Twitter?"

Lauren gave a big smile and grabbed her cell phone, "Yes I did, Tiff," she continued to press some buttons on her phone, "Hold on, let me find it," she said quietly.

Carmen looked perplexed, "What Top Ten list?" Lauren ignored her, so Tiffany answered proudly.

"Lauren and I made a list of the prettiest girls at Wilson," Tiffany smiled to herself, "We figured that whichever girls did not make the list will suck up to us now so that they could be considered for it next time."

"Ooo, creative!" Carmen said to Tiffany in much approval. Tiffany put her hand out for a catty high five.

Moving her hair out of her face again, Lauren finally shouted, "I found it!"

"Let's hear it then," said Tiffany Rodgers.

"Okay, so at ten I put Gwyneth H, then Jessica R, Victoria L, Hayden Y, Amber L, Amber J, Ayla F, Neisha T, Bryanna W, and tied for number one are the one and only T.L.Cs," Lauren recited, looking at her friends to see if they liked who made the list.

A wicked grin appeared slowly on Tiffany's face, "Do you understand how pissed Neisha is going to be, knowing that her BFF is prettier than her?"

"What about how Shaniquia, Lynda, or none of their girls not even make the list?" Carmen added, mimicking Tiffany's facial expression.

Lauren put her hand up to her mouth and faked an apologetic look, "Oops!"

The three girls laughed while Lauren posted the list to both Facebook and Twitter.

"I don't know about you guys, but I for one cannot wait to get to school tomorrow," Tiffany coolly said.

"Hey, what time is it?" Carmen asked her friends.

This time Tiffany ignored her, so Lauren gave her the answer, "Five-thirty."

"Oh, okay."

"Why did you wanna know?" Tiffany asked.

Carmen gave the girls her gorgeous smile, "I have a date with Allen tonight."

"Oh," Tiffany replied.

"Oh?" said Carmen, not really expecting that reaction from her girl, "What is that supposed to mean?"

"I mean, how long do you expect this 'relationship' with you and Allen to last? Seriously."

Carmen folded her arms over her chest, "What does that have to do with anything?"

Lauren suddenly pretended to gain a fascination with the five dollars her step dad gave her, not wanting to be in the middle of the discussion.

"It has to do with everything. You're dating Torean's clone. Do you not understand that? We all see the way Torean treats women on a regular basis, so what makes you think that Allen is really going to want to be in a relationship with you for too long? He has a reputation to maintain, just like all of us. And being in a long-term relationship is not in the job description," Tiffany told Carmen, rolling her neck the whole time she gave her speech.

Carmen opened her mouth in shock, "Why do you hate on me Tiffany? I finally found a boy who isn't a cheater, a liar, or a bad boy, and here you go trying to make my relationship seem like less than what it is. If you weren't so busy judging females on their looks, you would have noticed that Torean is in a relationship as well, so if Allen is his clone like you claim, then him and I really are the real deal."

Tiffany rolled her eyes and looked over at Carmen, "I've heard some things about your little boyfriend."

"Heard what?" Carmen asked hesitantly.

"Tiffany don't," Lauren finally interrupted.

"No," said Carmen, very curious now, "Tell me."

"You know what, since you really want to know," Tiffany said, giving Lauren a sneaky look, "I'll tell you what I heard from Torean Hudson himself," she said to Carmen.

"What is it?"

"Torean told me that Allen was being initiated into the Clique Boys."

"Umm, I'm going to go call Brian and thank him for the money he uuh, gave me," Lauren hurriedly told her friends, jumping out of the hot tub and rushing into her house, wanting to be anywhere else instead of by Carmen and Tiffany when a fight broke out.

Carmen sat in the tub and sat in silence for a while, "Well…is that all you had to tell me?"

Tiffany looked at her as if she was stupid, but thought better of it and replied, "Yeah. That's all."

Carmen laughed rudely at Tiffany, "So your way of making me not want Allen anymore is by telling me that he's being considered for the biggest group in our class? Only solidifying him as one of the most popular guys in our grade?"

Tiffany gave her a fake grin, "Yeah, I guess I don't really have any dirt on Allen to use against him after all."

"Of course you don't," said Carmen, "because Allen is a sweet guy who treats me with respect. We are going to be together for a long time, and you're just gonna have to deal with it," Carmen climbed the stairs to get out of the hot tub, "Well; I have a date to get ready for. I'll tell you all about it later tonight," Carmen strutted out of the indoor pool and passed Lauren on her way out. Lauren went back into the warm water with Tiffany, a look of confusion on her face.

"Why is she not mad?" Lauren asked.

Tiffany snickered, "Carmen's too busy having her head in the clouds to know that she's about to be made a fool out of."

Lauren bit her lip apprehensively, "She doesn't know about the sex tape does she?"

Tiffany slowly shook her head, "She doesn't have a clue."

"Oh jeeze, this isn't going to be good at all," Lauren sadly said. She reached over and picked up her cell phone, completely dropping her mournful expression, "Hey. You wanna see what people thought of our Top Ten list?"

"Of course! Let's check it out," Tiffany excitedly smiled. Carmen was one of Tiffany's best friends, but Tiffany's cutthroat attitude could not allow herself to want to be nice to Carmen once she got defensive about Allen. If Carmen did not want to listen to her, Tiffany was perfectly fine with letting Carmen find out what was in store for her the hard way.

TOREAN HUDSON & BRYANNA WILLIAMS
Wednesday, 7:00pm ~WILL'S DINER

Wills Diner was the place that Wilson High teenagers went to eat, chill, and have fun. It was full of flat-screen TV's, BET's latest music, and the coolest kids who went to Wilson. Even though there was not a huge sign that said you had to be known by the owner, who used to be MVP of the Golden Lion's basketball team back in the day, everyone knew it. That was exactly why Torean Hudson wanted to take his girl there; two popular people at the most popular place in town. The mood couldn't have been any better than that.

"Hey Torean. How's it goin'?" Will, the owner of the restaurant asked when Torean and Bryanna walked through the door.

Torean leaned his head in Bryanna's direction and replied, "You know man, just tryna have a good time."

"I feel you. I feel you," Will said nodding his head, trying to stay hip. He led them over to an empty booth near the back of the restaurant. The two of them sat down across from one another and began scanning their menus in silence. A few minutes later, the waiter, a fat, light-skinned boy, came through to take their orders.

"Imma have the nachos, but without jalapeños, and a strawberry lemonade," Torean told the waiter, then handed him back the menu.

"And you?" the waiter said, winking enticingly at Bryanna.

Bryanna slyly rolled her eyes at his gesture and told him, "I'll take a small plate of French fries with a Mountain Dew."

"Coming right up," he said while taking the menu out of Bryanna's hand, but not before rubbing his chubby fingers across hers.

When the waiter walked away, Torean burst out laughing.

"Ugh! What are you laughing at?" Bryanna asked Torean, still grossed out by getting hit on by that wanna-be Fat Joe.

"Why are you actin' like you didn't like ol' boy tryna get at you?" he joked.

Bryanna replied sarcastically, "Oh yeah. I liked it, but I just didn't want to hurt your feelings by flirting back with him."

"Really now?"

"Mmhmm," Bryanna answered with a smile, not looking over at her boyfriend.

The waiter came back with their drinks. He placed Torean's down roughly, making some of his lemonade splatter over the table. But when he gave Bryanna her soda, he placed it down carefully, even putting a coaster on the bottom of it.

"Aww thanks," She cooed to the waiter, "You're so helpful."

The guy blushed, "Just doing my job."

Bryanna smiled sweetly before he walked away, stumbling over himself.

Torean shook his head at his girlfriend, "Did you have to do that to him?"

"Do what?" she inquired innocently.

"Put that spell on him like that. You got him trippin' all over the place, and treating me like garbage."

Bryanna giggled.

"You are too fine for your own good ma," Torean said, wrapping up the discussion when he saw the food come out. Once again, his was dropped on the table, and Bryanna's was gently placed down. Torean made a mental note that this boy was definitely not getting a tip tonight.

The two of them ate and joked during their meal. Bryanna threw French fries into Torean's mouth, and Torean fed her what very little was left of his nachos. They were having a really good time, and they both knew it could only get better from there. After the plates were cleared away, the two of them sat in the booth, chilling.

"So what do you have planned this weekend?" Torean asked her.

Bryanna shrugged her shoulders, "I don't know. Probably just go to the mall with Neisha."

"Sounds like a plan. I'm probably going to just record some more demos with my boys, get high, then rap some more."

"Uh huh," Bryanna said, nodding her head slowly, "But you're forgetting one thing."

"What's that?" Torean couldn't think of anything else he was supposed to do this weekend.

After she saw that he was not catching the hint, she finally replied, "Me."

"Oh!" Torean said, opening his sexy mouth up, feeling silly that he forgot all about her, "We can definitely hang this weekend if you want to baby," he grabbed her hand and held it between his, "We can do anything you want to."

Bryanna smiled seductively up at him, "What about tonight?"

"Huh?" Torean asked, confused.

"Can we do what I want to do tonight?"

"Yeah—"

"Here's your check," the waiter said, throwing it down on the table.

Torean looked at the bill and laughed.

"What's wrong?" Bryanna asked.

Torean handed the leather book to her, "Check this out."

Bryanna scanned through the check. Everything looked normal to her. But then she looked at the bottom of the paper, where in what looked like chicken scratch, read:

555-7442. Call this number when you're ready to get with a real man.

"Oh. My. Gawd!," Bryanna said laughing. She ripped the note off the bottom of the receipt and put it in her pocket. Torean raised his eyebrows at her but didn't say anything. He put the money into the leather book and picked up on the conversation that the two of them were having before Fat Albert interrupted them.

"But anyway," he continued, "Yeah baby, what you wanna do tonight?"

She licked her bottom lip flirtatiously before saying, "You wanna come over to my house?"

Torean cleared his throat and smoothly tried to reply, even though excitement was clear in his voice, "I'm down."

They got up from the booth and hopped into Torean's Mercedes, driving to Bryanna's house. During the ride, Bryanna sat silently, playing with the charm bracelet on her wrist. She didn't even sing along to her favorite song "We Found Love" by Rihanna like she usually did.

"What's the matter?" Torean asked concerned, turning the music down.

Bryanna shook her head, "Nothing. I'm fine baby," She put on a fake smile that Torean saw right through. He really wasn't in the mood to have Bryanna scared. Tonight needed to be perfect. He did not want the night to be ruined by her being nervous. She'd had sex with guys before, so he didn't understand what the big deal was. But he did have that kind of effect on women. Unless…Unless she was not nervous about doing something. What if she was nervous about saying something? Saying three special words…

"The house is right here," Bryanna pointed, showing Torean a large house with a circle driveway and all the works. This place showed why she was queen of Wilson. Bryanna led him into her gorgeous house. They walked up a curved staircase that led to her room, and when she unlocked the door, his eyes opened wide. Torean had been in her house before, but he had never been granted permission to come inside her room.

Her room was all different shades of purple. From violet to lavender, purple was everywhere. She had a king-sized canopy bed, and a 24" flat screen computer on her desk. There was even a small hot tub next to the French doors, leading to the balcony.

"Damn," Torean said under his breath. His parents had money and everything, but damn this girl was loaded. He took a seat on her bed, watching her as she walked around her room, messing with stuff. The girl was seriously uneasy about something.

He bit his lower lip smoothly and asked, "What do you wanna do?"

She walked over to him and stood between his legs. Torean grabbed her by the waist, and she kissed him on the cheek. She pulled back slowly and Torean began to pull off her shirt, exposing her black Victoria's Secret bra. They continued to kiss each other while Bryanna pulled the white, V-neck shirt over Torean's head. She ran her hand over his 6-pack and started to kiss his collarbone. He leaned deeper onto the bed, and Bryanna laid on top of him in the straddle position.

Torean unbuttoned her jeans and slowly began to pull them down while they continued to kiss passionately with each other. Bryanna threw her Seven Jeans across her room and looked at him with hungry eyes.

"Baby?" Bryanna asked.

"Yeah?" Torean breathed, roaming her body with his hands.

"I...I..."

Torean waited for Bryanna to say what she was trying to get out of her mouth. He already knew what she wanted to say, but he could tell that she needed some encouragement. He started to kiss her around her neck, letting her feel on his muscles.

"I don't know how to say this Tor."

He continued to kiss her while he said, "It's okay baby. I love you too."

Bryanna pulled away from Torean and looked him directly in his face.

"Who said I was in love with you?"

Torean raised his eyebrows and scooted back from Bryanna, "What are you talking about? You were just about to say that you loved me a minute ago. You were stuttering and everything," Torean got defensive, "And the way you were acting during the ride over here."

Bryanna shook her head, "No Tor. I was nervous because I wanted to have sex with you, but I wasn't sure if you were ready. And I was trying to gain the courage to tell you that I don't think we should be in a relationship together. I just think that it would be better to only be friends with benefits right now."

"What?" Torean said, taken aback.

"C'mon Torean. You and I both know that girlfriend/boyfriend don't really fit you. I know you were only doing this because you thought this was the only way I would let you hit."

Now it was Torean's turn to start shaking his head. He grabbed her hand and said, "Baby; I wanted to be with you. Plain and simple"

Bryanna got off Torean, got his shirt from off the floor, and handed it to him.

"Now, you can either take your shirt and leave, knowing that this relationship is over, or you can throw the shirt back on the floor and have sex with me tonight, and the both of us go back to having things the way they used to be."

Torean looked down at his white-t and then back at Bryanna. He slowly put the shirt back on and zipped his pants back up. He walked towards the door of the bedroom and then looked back at Bryanna, who was standing there looking sorry for how things went down. It just pissed him off that she thought that less of him. What pissed him off even more was that when he said he loved her, it felt so right.

"Bre, I wanted to be with you," he truthfully said one more time, more to himself than to Bryanna, who was standing by her bed looking like she just lost out on something really special.

Torean left Bryanna's house feeling let down, hurt, and nervous. Now that he no longer had a girlfriend, there was no way that he would ever be able to win the bet.

ALLEN RIVERA   CARMEN SANCHEZ
Wednesday, 8:00pm ~ ALLEN'S HOUSE

Allen sprayed a dash of I AM KING on himself before rushing downstairs to go answer the door.

"Whoa," Allen said in awe. How could this girl possibly get any finer; he did not know. But here she was in living color, wearing a black mini skirt and a red tank top, with black stilettos on her feet. She wore her hair in loose curls and smelled like passion fruit body spray.

"Hi to you too, Allen," Carmen said, walking in the house. As she scanned around the house, it gave Allen time to pick his chin off the floor.

She took a seat on the couch, and Allen went into the kitchen to get the chocolate-covered strawberries out of the fridge. When he came back into the living room with them, Carmen covered her mouth, "Wow Allen. That is so sweet!"

Allen smiled and placed the plate of strawberries on the coffee table.

"Did your mommy help you do this?" she joked.

"Hahaha. Real funny."

Carmen grabbed Allen's hand while he took a seat beside her, "I was just joking babe."

"I know sexy," Allen replied, kissing her for a short time on the lips, "Now; you eat these, and I'll be right back," he said, motioning towards the strawberries.

Allen walked up the stairs and went into his bedroom. He checked to make sure his bedspread smelled fresh and that his Usher CD was in the radio. He walked a few feet across from his bed where his bookshelf was located. Between a Harry Potter and Steven King novel was a small video camera. Allen double-checked to see if his camera was filming at the right angle.

He felt like a complete jerk for what he was about to do to Carmen, but he wanted in the Clique Boys, and if this was what he had to do to get accepted, then that was the price he was willing to pay.

Allen checked once more to see if he had some condoms before going back downstairs to join his girlfriend in some chit-chat.

"So how you doin' beautiful?"

"I'm great. Besides having Tiffany annoy me today like she usually does; my day couldn't have been any better."

"Oh, so I didn't make your day good?" Allen asked, pretending to have his feelings hurt because he was not acknowledged by his girlfriend.

Carmen sarcastically rolled her eyes, "Allen, you made my day wonderful like always."

"Thank you babe," Allen said, kissing her on the cheek.

"Especially when you tried to steal all the camera time during the announcements," she finished smartly.

Allen ran his hand across his chin, like those wanna-be macks do, and said, "You already know I need my camera time. The people only watch the announcements 'cause I'm on 'em."

Carmen backed away from Allen in surprise, "Oh, is that right?"

He took a bite of strawberry, vigorously nodding his head yes.

"You're one funny guy, Allen Rivera."

Allen licked his lips, "And you're one sexy girl, Carmen Sanchez."

"You know that boy Cordell from the basketball team said the same thing to me?" Carmen said to him.

"I'm not surprised," Allen nonchalantly replied.

Carmen raised her arched eyebrows, "You're not jealous?"

Allen shrugged his shoulders, "What do I have to be jealous of? I'm the one who got you to be my girl, aren't I?"

Carmen laughed at Allen's cockiness.

"Baby," she said leaning in a bit closer to her man, "Why don't you do the comedy roasts anymore?"

He scratched his head while saying, "I don't have time for it anymore. I'm too busy trying to make a name for myself."

"But you already had a name."

He rolled his eyes, "Yeah, the class clown. Real cool."

"I thought it was cool. I liked you before you turned into this," Carmen said, touching his clothes, "I always thought you were a good person Allen."

Allen smiled at her compliment and stroked her cheek with the back of his hand. Hearing that from Carmen made Allen feel like all of his years of crushing were worth it. Carmen grabbed his hand and kissed every one of his fingers. He then began to French kiss her, leaning her back on the couch so that they could get more comfortable. Allen laid between Carmen's legs, which allowed him to feel up her bare thighs. She kissed Allen all over his neck and nibbled on his ear. Allen started to get so aroused that he pushed her deeper into the couch, now sliding his fingers in and out of Carmen. She began moaning into his ear until Allen finished the job.

Carmen leaned up and pushed Allen down on the couch, making him lay down on his back. He watched her with pure lust in his eyes as she pulled off her shirt revealing her beautiful breasts. They started kissing again, and Allen pulled away and took Carmen's hand.

"Come with me," he said, taking her to his room.

As soon as the door closed, Carmen ripped off her clothes, and Allen did the same. She lay in bed, looking like a pen-up, biting her lip sexually.

"Come here papí," she sensually said to Allen, taking a condom that was laying on his nightstand and waving it in his direction.

Allen climbed into the bed, but not before looking at the red light flashing on the camera.

Carmen propped herself up on her elbow, staring at Allen, who was lying down with his hands behind his head.

"Allen?" Carmen quietly asked.

"Huh?" he tiredly replied.

She rubbed her lips together and finger combed her hair in silence.

"Yeah Carmen?" Allen asked again.

"I love you."

Allen felt like his whole world stopped for a second, and reality finally struck him. He felt like the dumbest guy on the planet. The whole time he was busy worrying about making Carmen fall for him, he forgot how real those feelings would be. He couldn't believe she actually fell in love with him.

"Wha—What?" he stammered, propping himself on his bed.

Carmen gave him one of her gorgeous smiles, "I said that I love you Allen."

The light in her eyes caught Allen. She was seriously expressing her feelings to him. Like she was genuinely happy to have met Allen, and that she took appreciation for the relationship she was in. So many guys had done nothing but used Carmen, and she'd finally met a guy who respected her mind and body. She was not afraid to share her heart with him.

Allen grabbed the hand that Carmen wasn't leaning on, and looking into her happy eyes, he told her, "Carmen, I don't deserve your heart."

"Yes you do Allen."

"No I don't. This whole thing; me and you…is wrong."

Carmen shook her head in confusion, "What are you talking about Allen?"

Allen turned his head away from Carmen in shame.

"Tell me," she said, her voice trembling.

Allen closed his eyes for a second, preparing to tell her the truth. Once he opened them, he said, "Torean and I made a bet to see which one of us was a better player. We had to get a girl to fall in love with us, and whoever could get the girl to say it first would be the major player at Wilson."

Carmen thought to what Tiffany told her earlier. She held back her tears and said, "So all I was to you was a bet?"

"Wait. That's not all," Allen took a deep breath before telling her the rest, "After the first time we had sex, the guys wanted me to join the Clique Boys."

Allen continued, "But there was a catch. The thing was that I had to record myself having sex with a girl…And that girl was you."

Carmen slammed her fist down on the bed, letting tears fall down her face.

"How could you Allen? How could you make me feel like I'm important, like I can actually open my heart up to someone, and then do this to me?"

Allen tried to grab her hand again, but she pulled it away.

"Baby—"

"Don't you dare baby me!" she shouted, getting up from the bed and throwing her clothes back on, "You're just like all those other guys at school, walking around like they're a god, treating girls any way they want," Carmen paused, "No, actually you're worse than those boys. *You* used me to join a stupid group! I am so over you right now," Carmen said, wiping the tears off her face.

Allen hopped off the bed, trying to stop Carmen from leaving.

"Wait Carmen!" he shouted in frustration.

She stood before Allen with her arms folded across her chest and pain written on her face.

"I'm so sorry," Allen told his girlfriend, "I'm sure I can't apologize enough for what I did to you, but I'll try. I turned into this because I wanted to be with you. And I'll turn *back* into who I used to be, to be with you. I love you Carmen," Allen pleaded.

"I don't know if you've noticed this Allen," she said with no emotion in her voice, "but we're over," Carmen finished, pushing past Allen and began to walk down the stairs. Allen heard the front door slam, and he quietly closed the door to his bedroom. He went over to his jeans, as if he was in a daze, and pulled out his iPhone. With it, he sent a simple message to Torean:

The deals off…I'm done.

Allen walked over to his bookshelf and took the camcorder out from between the two books. He pressed the delete button on the video camera, deleting the video of him and Carmen. He silently climbed back into bed, pulling the covers as far over his head as he could. Allen lay in bed, with the beautiful scent of his ex-girlfriend still lingering on his pillow. Playing with Carmen's heart to be part of some high school clique was not worth it. He had the girl of his dreams right there in front of him, caring about him as much as he cared about her, and he ruined everything. Allen could never forgive himself for hurting Carmen the way that he did.

ALLEN RIVERA
Thursday, 11:20am ~ LUNCH

"Man you need to eat something,"

Patrick said to Allen as Allen sat at their table with his head down, and his lunch left untouched.

"I don't deserve food," Allen mumbled to his friend.

Patrick shrugged his shoulders, "I don't know why you're sitting here depressed. Carmen is the one who should be sad. No one told you to turn into an inconsiderate jerk just for popularity."

"And no one told you to be rubbing this crap in my face!" he shouted, jumping up from the table. He didn't know where he was about to go, but he needed to get the heck away from that boy. He could be too honest sometimes.

"Whoa dude! Looking up helps when you're walking," Torean joked to Allen when he knocked into him.

"Sorry man," Allen mumbled.

Torean gave Allen a good look over and saw how depressed he looked. He was wearing those stupid shorts and graphic shirts again. Torean remembered the text message Allen sent him last night, but he figured he was just talking about how he didn't make the video. Torean himself was bummed out over Bryanna, but he wouldn't dare let that show at school. He walked around with a fake smile and hollered at every girl who walked past him.

"Come here for a sec Allen," Torean motioned for Allen to the empty part of the cafeteria so that they could have a one-on-one.

Allen stood with Torean with his hands in his pockets and blood-shot eyes. Torean motioned for him to sit down.

"What's wrong man?" Torean asked.

"It's done. Me and Carmen. We're finished," he said in a monotone voice.

"What?" Torean said shocked.

"She dumped me, man."

"Why?" Torean curiously asked.

"She told me she loved me, and I couldn't live with myself. I came clean with the bet and the sex tape."

Torean put his hands up, "Wait, wait. So you're tellin' me that she told you she loved you, *and* you made the sex tape?"

Allen nodded his head somberly.

Torean could not believe this. This boy did everything. Technically, he was a major player *and* a Clique Boy. Was this really happening?

"But I'm done man," Allen said, burying his head in his tan hands, "I don't want to be a Clique Boy or a player."

Torean wanted to celebrate the fact that he no longer had any competition, but looking at the sad look on Allen's face. He honestly felt sorry for him.

"So what now?" Torean asked his hand on Allen's shoulder.

Allen replied, "You continue being a player with your girl, and I'll go back to doing what I do."

Torean shook his head, "Bre ain't my girl no more."

"What?" It was Allen's turn to get surprised.

"She didn't wanna be in a relationship anymore."

"Man, that's messed up," said Allen.

Torean smiled, "It's cool though. At least now I can go back to getting with all the women I want."

Allen shook his head at Torean's statement, "Naw man. I can tell you really cared about her. Just like I cared about Carmen. I love her Torean. And now I can never have her back."

Allen stood up from the table and walked away from Torean, leaving him there to ponder his thoughts.

I have to make things right.

***

Miserably walking nowhere in particular, Allen tried his hardest to get his mind off Carmen Sanchez. Out of nowhere, Allen jumped at the soft touch he got on his head.

"What?" he said, fixing his hair as he looked up to see who touched him. Once he realized who it was, he rolled his eyes and rudely mumbled, "Go away Lafonda, I'm not in the mood."

"Oh wow Allen, that's no way to talk to your ex-boo, now is it?" Lafonda casually said to Allen. He was about to reply with something mean, but the change in Lafonda's voice stopped him. Her usually heavy breathing and thick dialect was gone, and now replaced with a normal, girly voice. Allen finally picked his head up long enough to give her a good look over.

Her usual gelled ponytail, rotted teeth, mis-matched clothes, and lavender contacts were nowhere in sight. Instead, her eyes were her natural dark-brown color; she had a jet-black weave in her hair, and she wore clothes that finally made sense to the normal eye.

"Wow Lafonda, you look really nice," Allen kindly told her.

She flipped her hair over her shoulder and replied with a smile, "Thank you Allen. My new *boyfriend* helped to show me that I was beautiful just the way I was, but I decided to make this change for me," she spun around in a circle, showing herself off, "When I stopped eating those Big Texas, I dropped a little of weight, and everything else just seemed to fit into place."

Allen wasn't paying attention to anything she said after "My new boyfriend," "Who did you say you were dating?"

Lafonda smiled brightly, "Mitchell Tucker."

Allen could not believe it. This guy went from dating Carmen Sanchez to Lafonda Rice? "What was he thinking?" Allen accidentally said aloud.

"What was that?" Lafonda quickly asked back.

"Oh, nothing. I was just saying that I am very happy for you," lied Allen.

"You see Allen, both of us ended up with a happily ever after," Lafonda grinned.

Allen got depressed all over again, "Not me. Carmen ended things last night."

Lafonda put her hand over her heart, "Aww. I am so sorry to hear that. You mind telling me what happened?"

"I screwed up. I turned into someone whom I am not proud of," Allen answered.

Lafonda put her hand on his shoulder, knocking the wind right out of Allen, "Look at you, over here crying and moping around the school. Now, if you would've got with a real woman like me, you wouldn't be walking around crying and snotting all over the place."

"Lafonda," Allen warned.

"I'm just being honest. You went after a girl who was completely out of your league. You had to do so much stuff to try to impress her; I know because I did the same thing with you. But if you had just given in and let me treat you like you were good enough just the way you were; none of this would have happened," Lafonda told Allen.

Allen dryly replied, "So you're saying that if I dated you, everything would have been perfect?"

"Exactly," Lafonda answered, nodding her head once, "But you missed out. Now I have a man who treats me like I'm Beyonce. He also wants me to graduate this year, though that can't happen because my grades are so screwed up from messing with your big head. But next year, I'll graduate with Mitchell and continue to be happy."

Allen was getting bored hearing about Lafonda's happy new life. He wasn't content, so the last thing he wanted to do was listen to someone else's perfect relationship.

"Lafonda, I have to go."

"Okay," she said, "I hope everything works out with you and Carmen."

Allen gave a weak smile, despite that fact that he knew Carmen would never speak to him again, "I hope everything works out too."

TOREAN HUDSON
Saturday, 12:34pm ~ NORTHSIDE MALL

Torean walked around North Side Mall, looking for the Radio Shack that Allen worked in, when he saw her sitting there at Starbucks with her friends. The two girls were talking happily and animated, but the other girl looked like she wanted to be anywhere else but there.

He made his way over to the three girls, and tapped the somber one on her shoulder.

"Yes?" Carmen said, turning around to look at Torean.

"Can we talk?"

Tiffany and Lauren's ears perked up in anticipation.

"In private?" Torean finished.

Without a word, Carmen got up from her stool and walked over to an empty table in the middle of the food court. She sat there in silence, waiting for Torean to speak.

"I heard about you and Allen," he said.

"Uh huh," she said uninterested.

He continued, "You have to understand that this whole thing was my fault. I turned him into a player. I convinced him to do the bet. And I wanted him in the Clique Boys."

Carmen rolled her eyes, "Boy please. Allen's as much to blame as you are. He wanted to become a player. He dumbly accepted the bet. And he actually went through with making the video. He wanted all of this, and he didn't care about who he hurt in the process."

"This boy is in love with you Carmen. Can't you see that?" Torean pleaded.

"He was in love with what I was, and what I could give him," Carmen rudely replied.

"Oh, and you weren't?" said Torean, "You only started getting all in his face when he became a player, so don't you go throwin' that in his face."

Carmen's voice got louder, "You and I both know the rules. I could not date Allen when he was the way he was before all of this. He was not popular enough to hold my hand even. If I were to have dated Allen back then, no one would have respected me. But my decision did not mean that I never had feelings for him."

Torean tissed, "That's exactly why Allen turned into a player, because he knew that this was the only way you'd pay attention to him. Stop bullshitting around Carmen. If you cared about Allen before the change, then you would have been with him."

"Don't you dare tell me anything about caring for someone, Torean! I was in love with Allen, and he played me like I was some trick!" Carmen shouted.

Torean leaned back in his chair, "I know he hurt you. And I know you love him—,"

"*Loved* him," Carmen corrected.

"Oh, so you don't love him anymore?" Torean asked unbelieving, "That's why you're here at the mall that he works in, looking like you just found out you were gonna die?"

"I forgot he worked here," she lied.

Torean laughed, "Uh huh."

"But he hurt me Torean," Carmen said, "The one time I finally felt like I could trust someone, this is what he does to me."

"Do you still love him Carmen?" Torean asked, leaning in closer to her.

She nodded her head, wiping the lone tear off her cheek.

"Well, just get past the fact that he got caught up being someone he wasn't, and that he loves you, and that he made a horrible mistake," Torean added in again, "and that he loves you."

Carmen got quiet and fiddled her fingers.

"Did I mention that he loves you?"

"I just need time to think about this Torean," she stood up to leave, and Torean stood up with her. She moved in closer to Torean, and the two of them exchanged a hug. Once Carmen's head hit Torean's chest, all the emotions that she held in exploded, and she cried out all the hurt and confusion. Torean stood there and let her cry on him. Once she got herself together, she wiped her face with a napkin on the table.

"I have to think about this," she said thickly one more time before walking back into Starbucks to join her friends.

Torean fixed himself up, truly feeling sorry for what Carmen was going through, and continued on his way to finding Radio Shack.

***

Allen quickly turned around and headed in the opposite direction from which he saw Torean was coming, his heart beating fast, speechless.

How could I not have seen it? How could I not have known?

ALLEN RIVERA
Saturday, 7:58pm ~ ALLEN'S ROOM

"So Sick" was playing on Allens iPod, expressing all of his emotions. He laid in bed, still in shock from what he witnessed at the mall during his lunch break.

All he wanted to do was head down to the food court and grab himself something quick to eat, but when he reached the glass railing of the floor overlooking the food court, he spotted his friend Torean talking to this beyond beautiful chick.

For some reason, Allen couldn't take his eyes off Torean, watching, as if in slow motion, Torean sitting across from the girl while the two of them seemed to be talking about something. He squinted his eyes so that he could get a better look at the girl, but deep down inside, he knew that was unnecessary; Allen already knew that the girl was Carmen. He could tell from her shiny hair and curvaceous body.

What are they doing together? Allen remembered asking himself.

He still didn't move a single step as he watched the pair get up from their seats and embrace in a hug. Allen noticed the way Carmen's head was comfortably laying on Torean's chest, and how Torean was slowly rubbing his hands up and down her back, getting closer and closer to her butt.

Allen felt his already dented heart cave deeper into his chest. Any hope of him and Carmen getting back together instantly ended, all because his so-called friend, Torean, wanted to make a move on her; and what Torean wanted, he got. And from what Allen saw down there, Carmen wanted it to.

Couldn't the two of them have picked somewhere else to meet? They just had to hook up at the place he worked. Apparently, neither one of them had any respect for him nor his feelings. For them to embrace openly and flirt with each other the way they did, showed Allen that Carmen never truly cared for him, and that Torean was never his friend. All that mattered to Carmen was gaining more and more popularity, and all Torean wanted was to hook-up with one of the sexiest girls at Wilson High.

I guess they're both going to get what they wanted. Allen thought, disgust shown all over his face as he switched his iPod to play "End of the Road" by Boys II Men. Now this song really hit him deep.

This whole time that I've been confiding to Torean about how much I cared about Carmen, he's been sitting there, waiting for the right time to make his move. I bet he just couldn't wait for the two of us to break up so that he could run to her rescue and show her that 'funny man Allen Rivera' isn't half of the player Torean Hudson was.

Allen buried his head in his pillow. *And how could she just go for him? I thought she loved me. How could she do this to me?*

I should've known something like this would happen. T.L.C.'s and Clique Boys are too close with each other. I bet they've hooked up behind my back countless times, but today was the day they finally got caught. The way they always look at each other during the announcements, and Torean's always inviting her to his parties. How could I not have seen this coming?

Allen couldn't take listening to the heart-broken songs anymore, so he snatched his earphones out of his ears and threw his iPod across his room in frustration.

You know what? Allen continued to think. *I don't need to deal with this. It's obvious that Torean was just taking advantage of Carmen because she's so vulnerable. That's what Torean always does to these women. Always.*

He jumped at the sudden sound of his ring tone playing on his iPhone. Allen picked his phone up and saw that Torean was calling him. He rolled his eyes at the mere thought of talking to that fake friend of his, and shut his phone off.

I don't need him in my life. We're not boys; we're not friends...We're nothing.

Allen lay back on the bed in a miserable huff, trying with all his might to keep his ex-girl and his ex-friend out of his head.

TOREAN HUDSON
Monday, 7:30am ~ PARKING LOT

Torean sat in his Mercedes, once again dialing Allen's number. For what had to be the hundredth time, Allen hadn't answered his call. He tissed and continued to look out his car window for the appearance of Allen's Chevy.

After a few more minutes, it finally pulled in the parking lot.

Torean hopped out of his car and made a run for Allen. They hadn't talked all weekend, and all Torean wanted to do was tell Allen that there still was a chance for him to get back with Carmen.

Allen got out of his truck and quickly spotted Torean running towards him with this big, fake smile on his face. It made him want to vomit in his mouth.

He tried to get back in his car, hoping that maybe he could drive off in time and wait it out until the bell rang, but right as he was about to open the truck door, he felt someone grip his shoulder.

Damn. Allen turned around and looked the scheming bastard in his perfect face.

Torean smiled at him, "What's up man?"

Allen shrugged, "Nothin'."

"Oookay," Torean said, not quite feeling the way Allen was acting towards him. Someone had a major attitude.

"So, where have you been this weekend?" he continued, brushing off the weird vibe he was getting from his boy.

"Why?"

Torean squinted his eyes at Allen, confused at why he was acting like such a dick.

Allen rolled his eyes, not able to hold a conversation with this backstabbing boy, "I gotta go," he said to Torean, roughly bumping into Torean's shoulder as he walked away.

"What in the hell?" Torean said to himself. He tried to catch up to Allen to see what was wrong with him, but he was already in the school, amidst of the hundreds of students, and he couldn't spot him out.

That's how it went all day long; Torean would try to talk to Allen and see what his deal was, but Allen would brush him off as if he was some kind of bad habit. He couldn't get a word in during Spanish, and even when he tried to get at him during lunch, Allen picked his food up, threw it in the garbage, and walked out the cafeteria.

Torean had no clue what was going on with his friend, but it must be something big to wipe that goofy smile off his face and replace it with a look of pure disgust.

Once seventh hour rolled around; he walked into the announcement room, expecting only the worse. There was no way his day could end on a good note when one of his boys was mad at him.

ALLEN RIVERA
Monday, 2:50pm ~ SEVENTH HOUR

Torean smiled in Carmens gorgeous face,
"So how you holdin' up?"

She returned a weak smile, "I'm doing as well as I can. I'm still hurting though."

"Ugh," Allen shook his head as he looked on in torture as he watched Torean caress his girl's arm. That's *his* arm, and he was being completely disrespected.

Allen tried to get his mind off what he was witnessing by practicing what he had to say for the Spotlight, but he couldn't concentrate. Every time Torean smiled at Carmen, made her laugh, or touched her; Allen felt a piece of his heart break off.

Torean knitted his hand through Carmen's, "I know the two of you belong together; everyone can see that. You just need to stop running away from him Carmen."

"That's it!" Allen said, storming up to Torean. He grabbed him by his toned arm, the one that wasn't holding onto Carmen, "I need to get at you for a minute."

Torean looked down at the grip that Allen had on his arm and raised his eyebrows in surprise, "What's your problem man?" he said, yanking his arm away while walking into their dressing room.

Allen slammed the door behind him, "You think I'm going to just let you steal my girl like that? Huh?" Allen said, his anger rising higher and higher.

Torean cocked his neck at him, "Hold up Allen. What the hell are you talkin' about?" Torean couldn't believe how bold Allen acted.

"Man, you know what I'm talkin' about," Allen spat at him, "I saw you at the mall Saturday, running game on Carmen."

Torean finally understood why Allen was acting so rude to him. He shook his head while laughing at the situation.

"What man? So you think this is funny now?"

"No, no," Torean replied, still laughing at Allen, "Man, you got it all wrong. That Saturday, I went to the mall, looking for you so that we could find a way to get you back together with Carmen—"

Allen swatted his hand at Torean, "Whatever man. I don't have time for your lies. Tell me the truth for once in your life."

Torean leaned his back against the door of the room and continued, "Like I was trying to say, I came to the mall for you, but when I saw Carmen, I had to talk to her and see if there was anything that I could do to help the two of you."

Allen looked over at Torean, waiting for the rest of his explanation to continue.

"I talked to her, and she told me that you really screwed up. I tried to tell her that it was my fault that you made the sex tape, even the bet, but she still wasn't tryna hear it."

"What about that hug I saw the two of you share, or the fact that you guys were just holding hands a few minutes ago? None of that looked like you were trying to be my boy," Allen was unconvinced with Torean's story.

Torean answered quickly, "I was just comforting her. She is really hurt Allen. I know you can see that; I was only trying to make her feel better. There is absolutely nothing going on with Carmen and me."

"Damn," Allen cursed under his breath, finally believing Torean's story, yet mad that Carmen still was not willing to take him back.

Torean walked up to Allen and put both his hands on Allen's shoulders, "But look here, Carmen's still in love with you; she told me that herself. All she wants is time."

Allen looked at his friend and slowly nodded his head, "I'm sorry for doing you like that...I just didn't know what to think when I saw—"

"It's cool," Torean said, brushing the apology off, "Just know that when I say that we're friends, I mean it. I would never do some dirty mess like that man. You gotta know that."

"I know that bro."

"Aight. So you know what you have to do now right?" Torean asked.

Allen shook his head, "What?"

"Give your boy a play!" the two laughed and gave each other a dap. Torean let go of Allen's hand and made his way back to the door. He opened it, and once he was halfway out the door; he turned to Allen, who was still standing there and said, "And the next thing you have to do is give your girl some time to heal."

Allen looked at the serious Torean, and quietly watched him as he closed the door, leaving him there to think things through.

Allen decided to give Carmen exactly what she wanted:
Time.

ALLEN RIVERA
Monday, 3:17p.m. SOPHOMORE HALLWAY

Allen closed his locker and began to text Patrick, checking to see if he still wanted to play video games after school.

"Yo Allen!" Torean shouted from across the hall. Allen turned around and smiled at him, "What's up man?"

"Come over here for a second," Torean replied. The Clique Boys were gathering up their things to leave, a group of girls standing around them like always. Allen adjusted his Boston Celtics graphic tee as he made his way over to the crew.

"What's up Allen?" Drew asked Allen.

"Nothing. Just getting ready to go home," he answered, "What about you guys?" he hadn't spoken to the Clique Boys since he saw Torean at the mall, but he figured it was for the best. He was no longer a player, and he was no longer being initiated for the Clique Boys, so there was no real reason for him to be hanging around them all the time like he used to.

Ricky said to him, "We're about to head over to Govern Park and do the usual."

"You wanna join us?" Marcus added.

Allen could not believe it. The Clique Boys still wanted to hang out with him even though he wasn't Mr. Popular anymore. And they weren't just following the lead of Torean Hudson, because he was not the one who invited him. Allen guessed that he really did make real friends with these guys after all.

"So you coming or what?" Torean asked.

Just then, Allen's phone vibrated. He pulled it out of his pocket and read the text from Patrick:

I'm leaving the locker room right now. Hope ur ready to get ur butt kicked in Madden!

Allen smiled to himself and then looked up at his other friends, "I have a better idea. How about we all, and my best friend Patrick, go over to my place and play some Madden 2k12? There will be tons of food and a 48" television with crazy speakers."

Torean put his hand up to stop him from talking, "You had me at tons of food. We can go," the rest of the guys nodded their heads in eager agreement. The girls they were with had a let-down expression on their face, and drifted off, seeing that the Clique Boys no longer needed them anymore.

"Awesome!" Allen said, giving Torean a play. Patrick came up to Allen and said, "You ready to go?"

"Hold on a second," Allen said to his friend, "Patrick, I never got the chance to introduce you to these guys when I was being a terrible friend to you, but I just want you to meet the Clique Boys."

Patrick looked confused, but went along with it.

"Torean, this is Patrick, and Patrick this is Torean," Allen said. He did the same thing for Ricky, Marcus, and Drew. After the introduction to everyone, each one of the Clique Boys gave Patrick a play.

Allen continued speaking again, "I hope it's cool, but I invited them over to play some Madden with us."

Patrick laughed, "So that's why all those girls were leaving?"

Ricky and Drew laughed, "Yeah. You mind if we come over with you guys?"

Patrick looked at Allen and then over at the popular guys, "Only on one exception."

"And what's that?" Marcus asked.

Allen started to get nervous.

"You bring those girls over to Allen's house too. Madden's not Madden without a group of beautiful ladies to cheer me on!"

Torean and the rest of the guys started laughing, "Man, I like you! But we all know that Torean Hudson is a beast at 2k12."

Patrick swatted his hand at Torean, "Yeah, whatever," The six boys walked down the hallway talking trash to each other the entire time, until they reached the parking lot to get into their cars.

"Alright man, we're going to follow you to your place," Torean coolly said to Allen.

"Sounds like a plan," Allen replied, him and Patrick making their way towards his Chevy.

"Those guys weren't half bad," Patrick said to his best friend, opening the red car door.

"I figured there was no point in separating my friends," Allen told him.

"Way to be noble man," Patrick sarcastically said to Allen, "All I know is that they better make sure those girls come over."

Allen laughed at Patrick, "I thought you weren't interested in girls right now."

"I'm not," said Patrick plainly, "But that doesn't mean they can't be interested in me."

Allen gave Patrick a high five, chuckling, "And that's why you're my best friend."

TOREAN HUDSON
Tuesday, 1:30pm ~ BIOLOGY

"Can someone pass me the notes?"

Torean said to the people at his lab table.

"Here," Bryanna said, passing him the notes.

Torean passed the notes back to Bryanna, "Can anyone else pass me the notes?"

Drew attempted to hand the notes to Torean, but Bryanna snatched them out of his hand.

"Here you go Torean," she said, handing the notes back to Torean.

He rolled his eyes at her and took the notes while saying, "Do you trust me with these notes, or do you think I just wanna hook up with them?"

Bryanna sucked her teeth, "How many times am I going to have to apologize? I was wrong for not trusting you, okay. I'm just not in the mood for a relationship right now Tor."

Every day since Wednesday night, Torean had been treating her like she was a monster, and she has been letting all the comments slide, but she was not in the mood for that today.

"I don't wanna be with you either Bryanna," Torean rudely retorted.

Bryanna laughed, "You weren't saying that Wednesday night."

Neisha and Drew inconspicuously walked away from the two before the conversation took a turn for the worst.

"Wednesday night I thought you cared about me. But apparently you didn't," Torean replied sourly.

Bryanna squinted her eyes at him, "What is this really about Torean?"

Torean squinted his eyes right back at her and answered, "You already know what this is about."

Bryanna walked over to the side of the lab table where Torean was standing. He moved back from her a couple of feet. She asked him again, "What is this about?"

Torean blew out some air and replied, "It's about the fact that all I wanted to do was be with you, but all you could do was think about what my motives were. If you didn't trust me, you shouldn't have agreed to be my girlfriend."

"I wanted to be your girlfriend because part of me did trust you. You were a good boyfriend and there was never any drama when we dated. I also have to see a side of you that I'm sure not too many girls have seen. But you have to understand that it's hard for me to look past the fact that you're a Clique Boy and what your reputation is."

"Whatever, Bryanna. I don't have time to listen to this," Torean turned away from her, and began copying down the notes.

Bryanna grabbed the arm he was using to write, making him look at her, "Tell me this then: When you said you loved me, did you really mean it?"

Torean shrugged his shoulders, "Me telling you the answer to that won't make you come back to me."

"No, it won't," Bryanna honestly answered, "But I just want to know if you really meant what you said," she paused for a second, "I have to know."

Torean looked at the hopeful look in Bryanna's eyes and thought for a moment. He thought about their kisses, her personality, and her heart. He, himself, had been questioning whether or not he genuinely meant what he said to her, or if the player in him was just trying to get the job done.

Finally, he answered, "I don't know what I feel anymore Bryanna. But I can say that I wouldn't have wasted my time with you if I didn't think you were special."

Bryanna slowly nodded her head while she let Torean's words sink in. He might have not really loved her when he told her those words, but she was sure that if their relationship had continued, things would have been different. It was just hard to know what was in his heart when he didn't speak it.

"Are you happy with your answer?" Torean asked her.

"Are you happy with us?" Bryanna asked curiously.

"I have no choice but to be happy with it."

Bryanna placed her hand on his shoulder and said, "You're a good-looking guy Torean. I'm sure you can find a new girl in a second."

"I know I'm fine. It's just that…" Torean stopped himself from being vulnerable with her, "Let's just drop it."

Bryanna rose her eyebrows, "You sure?"

"I'm cool," Torean replied, nodding his head.

"So we're friends?" Bryanna asked cautiously.

Torean pulled her in for a hug, a fake smile plastered on his handsome face.

"Just friends."

CHARMANE WHITE

ALLEN RIVERA
Monday, 2:25pm ~ ANNOUNCEMENTS

"Can we ever start the announcements on time?" Kayla shrieked to the teens standing around her.

"We're here!" Torean and Allen shouted, sliding into their chairs. Carmen was already in her chair, looking like a Latina goddess, as usual.

"Alright. Cameras roll in 5.4.3.2…" Kayla shouted to Ricky and the newscast.

The opening music started, and usually everyone was hyper and ready to start the show, but since the tension between Carmen and Allen had not yet gone away, they'd just been putting on a fake smile lately for the announcements' sake.

"Wussup Wilson High. It's time for your morning announcements hosted by yours truly, Torean Hudson."

"And me, Carmen Sanchez."

"And don't y'all forget about the Wilson High Spotlight with Allen Rivera," Allen said, gazing over at Carmen the entire time he introduced himself.

Carmen noticed him looking, and she cleared her throat uncomfortably and began the school news.

"There will be a mandatory meeting for the members of the debate team after school in Mr. Kenford's classroom."

"If anyone is interested in donating winter clothes to the Salvation Army, please place your items in the red boxes placed in front of the school. It's going to be a cold winter, so please help those in need," Torean said.

"That just about does it for news, so let's go back to Allen—I mean Torean, for sports," Carmen stammered, her face turning pink.

Torean glanced at Allen before giving the sports news.

"The girls' basketball team faced their first loss of the season. But it's all right. You ladies are fine as hell anyways."

"Torean!" Kayla shouted.

He continued, "Now it's time to see what's for lunch."

"Umm," Carmen mumbled, "look forward to enjoying Taco Tuesday!" she tried to put some enthusiasm on the end of it, but no one bought it.

"It's Allen's turn for the Wilson High Spotlight," She said, not caring if she was enthusiastic or not.

Allen cut his eyes at her while his theme music played. Once it stopped, he began.

"Today the spotlight shines on…" he began to trail off.

"Allen!" Kayla yelled, starting to get frustrated.

He shook his head to get his mind back on track, "Today the spotlight shines on Carmen Sanchez."

Everyone looked at each other in confusion. Chris Bennett was supposed to be given the spotlight today.

"Allen?" Carmen whispered to him.

He continued on, "This beautiful girl has been stuck in my head since I first laid eyes on her in elementary school. And now she has captured my heart. Right now, she's hurting because I did something horrible to her, but I hope that one day soon she'll be able to forgive me for what I did. Carmen Sanchez, I love you."

Torean attempted to fill the awkward silence that ran throughout the screening room by closing out the announcements.

"Well, that does it with your morning announcements with me, Torean."

"I love you Allen."

"And ya boy A. Rivera—wait. What?" he said quickly, turning his head to Carmen.

She stood up and smiled at Allen, "I said I love you."

Allen felt as if his world made sense again. There was no better feeling than what he was feeling right now.

"Can you say that *one* more time?" he said, wrapping his arms around her waist, pulling her in closer to him.

Carmen wiped the happy tears off her face and said, "I love you Allen Rivera."

Allen smiled, and they exchanged a kiss as if they were in private behind a closed door, not like they were in front of a camera and a bunch of other people. They kissed like two people in love.

Torean's face hurt from how hard he was grinning at the two. He turned back into the camera and said, "And don't forget, at Wilson High, we might tell the news, but people like them," he said moving his head towards Allen and Carmen, "Make the news."

ALLEN RIVERA

Tuesday, 10:20am ~ SPANISH

"Everyone open up your books to page 103."

Groans erupted throughout the Spanish II classroom.

"Do you guys ever shut up?" Mr. Brunning said to his students, annoyance clear in his voice.

Carmen laughed at the teacher. He could be such a jerk sometimes.

Allen, who was sitting right next to her, whispered, "You are so sexy when you laugh."

"Gracias," She winked at him.

He kissed her tenderly on her sweater-covered shoulder.

"Allen, do you mind taking a few minutes away from your *shortie* and actually pay attention in this class?" Mr. Brunning rudely spat at Allen.

Allen rolled his eyes at the teacher in return, "China Man, please. I speak better Spanish than you do."

The class exploded in laughter.

"Ha, ha, ha!" Brunning sarcastically laughed.

"You better ha, ha your way back over to teachin' this class," Allen warned.

Carmen rubbed Allen's forearm, "Baby, be nice."

Mr. Brunning was tired of Allen always picking a fight with him in his own class. He was the teacher, and Allen was the student. It was about time he learned his place, "Why don't you go cook yourself a burrito or something Mr. Rivera?"

The whole class got quiet at the teacher's words. Everyone knew that Brunning absolutely hated Allen, but to be a grown man, and to go racial on Allen. That type of behavior can lead to nothing else except—

Torean looked over at Allen and shouted, "Get 'em!"

"Get yo' big stank butt outta here, smellin' like catfish!"

"Get 'em!"

"Get yo' Kung Fu Panda lookin' ass outta here!"

"GET 'EM!"

"Look at yo' pants! Them tight behind pants all up yo' crack!"

Everyone was laughing and pointing at Mr. Brunning's pants.

"Get yo' little pencil joint lookin' behind outta here!"

You could hear the classroom's laughter throughout the hallway.

"Get 'em!" Torean shouted again.

Mr. Brunning slammed his eraser down on the ground in anger. "You and you!" he shouted at Torean Hudson and Allen Rivera, so angry that a vein was popping out of his neck, "Pack your stuff and get out of my classroom. NOW!"

Allen and Torean snickered while Carmen shook her head at Allen, not being able to conceal her laughter all the way, and the two of them exited the room and made their way to the principal's office.

Taking his usual seat on the bench outside the office, Allen said to Torean, "Man, I sure haven't done this in a while."

Everything was good with Allen Rivera. He made new friends, had a beautiful girlfriend, and his jokes were getting better every day. He couldn't believe that just a while ago he was fantasizing about what it would be like to be a player; how cool he'd be and all the amazing things that would come with the title.

CHARMAINE WHITE

But through all the girls, friends, parties, and drama, he found out one thing:

Being himself felt so much better.

The End.

READING GROUP DISCUSSION QUESTIONS

1. Are the T.L.C.'s a group of girls that can be found in any high school? If a group of girls similar to the T.L.C.'s go to your school, is their behavior frowned upon or looked at as cool?

2. Do you think Patrick was too easy on Allen for ditching him to hang out with the Clique Boys on a regular basis? Would you ever leave your best friend behind if you had the chance to become friends with the most popular group at school?

3. After seeing the way Carmen fell for Allen after he transformed into a player, can you agree with her actions? Why do you think most girls are attracted to players?

4. Allen seemed to be very close to his parents, especially when he had a talk with his father about sex. How comfortable are you with talking to your parents about relationships and sex? Do you even think that is a subject your parents would want to discuss?

5. After getting to know the character of Lafonda Rice, do you feel that she was good enough to get a guy like Mitchell Tucker? Do you think Lafonda was crazy, or simply just a girl who fell for all the wrong guys?

6. Was Allen a more likeable character when he was the class clown, or when he was a ladies' man?

7.   At times in the book, the Clique Boys appeared to do whatever Torean told them to, no questions asked. Do you think that the other Clique Boys are scared of him, or do they just respect the fact that Torean is the leader of the group? Within your group of friends, do you think of yourself as the leader or just another member?

8. The various cliques of Wilson High include an ethnically diverse group of people. Would you say the same goes for you and your group of friends? If not, what might the reasons be for that?

9.   It seemed as if Neisha Thompson just could not avoid Marcus Hamilton this semester. Do you predict that the two will make amends for Marcus' scheming behavior? Do you have an ex at your high school who you try to avoid, but they always seem to be around? How does that make you feel?

10. If you could be any character in Player Hater, who would you be? Why?

WAHIDA CLARK PRESENTS
YOUNG ADULT
BEST SELLING TITLES

Under Pressure by Rashawn Hughes

The Boy Is Mines! By Charmaine White

Ninety-nine Problems Gloria Dotson-Lewis

Sade's Secret by Sparkle

ON SALE NOW!

www.wcpyoungadult.com

60 Evergreen Place Suite 904 East Orange NJ 07018

973.678.9982

WAHIDA CLARK PRESENTS

Y.A.
YOUNG ADULT

NINETY-NINE
PROBLEMS

A Young Adult Novel BY
GLORIA DOTSON-LEWIS

WAHIDA CLARK PRESENTS

UNDER PRESSURE

Y.A.
YOUNG ADULT

A YOUNG ADULT NOVEL BY

RASHAWN HUGHES

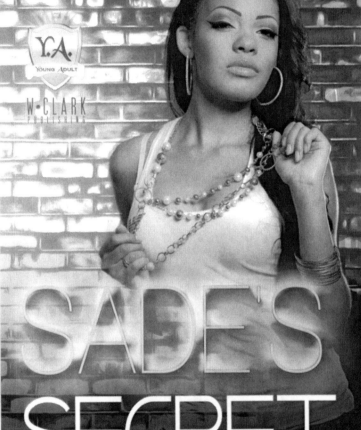

WAHIDA CLARK PRESENTS

SADE'S SECRET

A Young Adult Novel By

SPARKLE

WAHIDA CLARK PRESENTS

Y.A.
YOUNG ADULT

THE BOY IS MINE!

A WILSON HIGH CONFIDENTIAL

A YOUNG ADULT NOVEL BY

CHARMAINE WHITE

CPSIA information can be obtained
at www.ICGtesting.com
Printed in the USA
LVOW10s1919280217

525690LV00016B/204/P